DARK WAS THE MORNING

AND OTHER STORIES

JENNIFER M. BALDWIN

Published in 2025 by Phoenix and Fox Emporium
First paperback edition, 2025

Phoenix and Fox Emporium
www.phoenixandfoxemporium.com

Dark Was the Morning and Other Stories/Jennifer M. Baldwin — 1st ed.
Paperback ISBN: 978-1-959362-04-3

———

CONTENTS

DARK WAS THE MORNING

My eyes were crusted shut. The cool, pale dawn was stirring, but I could not see it. I could see nothing but the black and red starbursts that flashed across the insides of my lids. My massive eyelids, and my massive eyes. What they had seen in this world. It would make fleshy men shiver. It would send out cries from the mouths of human mothers. It would terrify even my brethren.

I knew I had to tear apart the bitter, yellow mucus that had hardened and sealed my eyelids, but the thought of the pain that came with such rending made me shiver a little. A cowardly old relic. That's what I was. I stretched my oak-like legs over the tiny rings of gold, letting them chafe my scales and rub off the dead skin. I unfurled my tail. It ached, but it felt good to stretch the old thing and snap it back and forth, listening to the gentle tinkling of gold and gems and silver cups that made music as my appendage swept across them.

Finally, I tore my eyes open. Bits of filmy crust fell into my open eyes, and my sight blurred for a moment as I tried to make sense of the waking daylight. The mouth of my cave yawned wide. It was a huge doorway that let me see the white-peaked mountains and towering pines that made up my realm. Winter was approaching soon; the paleness of the sun promised it. Soon I would dive deeper into the cave, into the waiting bowels of earth, to ride out the winter in peaceful slumber.

But autumn was not over yet. A few more flights, a few more feasts awaited my old bones and sagging skin. The cool morning air would dispel the last bits of crust from my eyes. Then I could hunt, and perhaps find some satisfaction in this lonely existence.

Oh, how old had I become! To wake merely for food and the tentative hope that something of interest might happen to me today. Alas, I knew better. Nothing ever happened to me anymore. One day soon, I am sure that I shall wake and the crust that covers my eyes will have spread to cover my whole self, entombed forever in the phlegm of old age. To rip such a cage open will be too excruciating to contemplate. Better to sleep forever and not suffer.

But the morning had come, and the daylight. My stomach cramped with hunger. In the far distance, past the arrowed pines, storm clouds bubbled across the sky and promised cold autumn rain. Prey would scurry and hide from that rain if I did not take flight soon. With one last stretch of my tail, I heaved my legs from my mounds of gold, listened as the pieces cascaded like a waterfall, and soared into the merciless world.

———

An old mare, that was all I could find in the far valley. She had wandered from the herd, and either through stubbornness or in folly, she realized too late that she could not outrun the beat of my wings. One of the wild breed that roamed these lands, she had once been a noble creature, but her flesh hung loose upon her frame, and her hair was brittle as dried grass. It had been a hard season for her, as hard as my own, perhaps. So I took her into my jaws and rescued her from the harsh winter to come, freeing her from the starvation that surely would have stolen her life. Taken thus, she was ennobled again, sustenance for my ravenous body.

Still, such a paltry meal did not satiate my hunger. Few things ever did.

I flew back to my cave, sobered by the creak in my old bones and the strain my wings had already taken from such a short morning flight. And yet, when I returned to the gaping maw of my home, I was further chastened to find it occupied by no less than a haggard dwarf polishing his battle axe while seated upon my hoard.

I did not hesitate upon that threshold, but slid into my cave and raised my head to strike this fool who dared intrude upon my barrow.

To his credit, he did not flinch, and it was that indifference or haughty courage which stayed my jaws and made me decide to parlay with him instead. For even as old as I was, my curiosity was like that of a young drake.

"What meaning is this, coming to my cave as bold as brass?" I asked.

The dwarf didn't speak. The steady, grating sound of his whetstone was his answer.

"You have been favored by good fortune," I continued. "My first meal this morning was paltry and my stomach still yearns for fresh meat. Ready yourself as I open my jaws again, and you shall be the next morsel in the mouth of Azragzigal, the mighty. A glorious fate, indeed!"

I was ready to bestow this honor when the dwarf surprised me again. He smiled.

"Mighty?" He almost laughed. "Is that what you call that sack of bones you drag around on those flimsy wings?"

The effrontery was most amusing. I had not parlayed with a foolhardy warrior in nearly five centuries. I allowed myself a melody of laughter in answer. It was like the sound of rocks crashing down the mountain.

But still, my intruder did not blanche.

"Now that I've come here, I'm not sure I want to do it[Perhaps this doesn't mean what we think it means... maybe the dwarf is talking about telling Azragzigal about his mother]," he continued. "What would be the point? I almost feel sorry for you."

"Am I really so pathetic?" I grinned, rows of teeth gleaming with my venomous saliva. "Shall you take pity upon Azragzigal?"

"Pity? I don't know about that. More like a lack of will. What's the point?"

"The point might be to evade death. Yours, I mean."

"Will you really? Somehow I doubt it." He kept sharpening his blade.

I, in turn, did not let my muscles relax. I may be slower now than in my younger days, but I have faced down many a fool who calls himself "dragon-slayer," and I know all their feints and trickery. This business of lacking the will, of questioning one's purpose. I had heard it before, and I'm sure I will hear it again. I wonder if it makes them feel better to pretend their task isn't predicated on bloodlust, to imagine they are simply doing such unpleasantries because they have no other choice, because the poor folk who suffer under my wings are terrorized with fear.

"And why do you doubt it? Are not my teeth sharp? And is not my sack of bones, as you call it, looking rather starved? I tell you, dragon-slayer, I am ravenous."

"I could use some breakfast myself."

Finally, he stopped sharpening his axe and set it down, the heavy iron head clanking against a dozen small silver coins. A fraction of my vast hoard, but still, it annoyed me to see him treat it thus. He sat upon the pile of coins and cups and gems from empires innumerable as if he sat upon a stool at the tavern.

Admittedly, the lack of fear from this dwarf continued to rouse my curiosity. From his large leather sack, he pulled forth a wedge of cream-colored cheese and nibbled on the edge of it like a mouse.

"You won't eat me because you're as lacking in will as I am." When he talked, a few spittles of cheese dribbled from the corners of his gray-bearded mouth.

"I ate a wild mare not one hour ago," I returned.

He shrugged. "That's not what I mean, and you know it."

"Tell me what you mean, then. I am rather slow in my dotage. Enlighten an old wyrm."

"You said it. You're old. And so am I. When's the last time you really hunted? Not wild mares or roe deer, but whole villages, kingdoms even? When's the last time you set forth your flame?"

"I destroyed the people who settled this land. Long ago my flames licked their flesh from their bones."

The dwarf nodded, wiping a fleck of cheese from the corner of his broad lips. "Aye. You did. Long ago. And now what have you become?"

I'd had enough. Lifting my neck with a stiff strain, I loosened my jaws. The links of his mail shirt would grind to gritty dust between my teeth, but at least his blood would run hot down my dry throat. I thought I saw him blanche as my mouth widened, his foolish confidence starting to crack.

But when I tried to lunge forward, I found myself unable to move. Not by any physical impediment but by something else. A kind of heaviness that was not in my limbs or my neck but in the recesses of my heart. I was angry with him, yes, but I could not bring myself to act. I did not want to.

My body settled back down into my hoard with a winded, sagging thud, and I closed my jaws and sighed. Steam as hot as molten rock rose from my nostrils and clouded the high ceiling of my cave. I could see the dwarf almost coughing from the smoke, but he held his composure.

"They deserved it," I said at last. "A wicked people. Greedy and cruel to one another. I did them a mercy by destroying them."

"Greedy, eh?" he said.

"They wanted my treasure."

"Your treasure?" He raised an eyebrow.

I should have roasted him right then and there, but I did not. Instead, I let more steam come clouding out of my snout.

Let him choke on it and be poisoned by the air. I would still achieve my aim but with less exertion.

"What do you call a hoard of gold and silver that has been with me for over a thousand years?" I asked. "Is it not mine?"

"It's in your possession, yes. But it wasn't always."

"That is an impossible standard," I growled, if such a wheezing, hacking sound could be called thus. I was growing more and more strained as the parlay went on. "No treasure stays in one creature's possession always. Unless one is a jeweler or goldsmith, and even then, those makers must get their precious metals and gems from miners. And even the miners must carve the stuff from the rock of the earth."

"So all this belongs to the earth, I think," said the dwarf, gesturing to my hoard.

"Perhaps," I smiled, "which is why I house it in a cave. To keep it close to its roots. But what would man or dwarf do with such riches? Give them away as payment or bribery, store them up in strange vaults in castles or keeps? At least I let them sit upon the earth and be content. I deal not in base trading nor commerce."

"Commerce keeps some men fed."

"That is not my concern. I am older than grasping merchants and covetous kings."

"You killed children," the dwarf said, his voice as even and unmoved as before. He said it as if he were telling the time of day. "And mothers and the feeble and old. Were they wicked, I wonder? Greedy and cruel?"

"Children grow up, and mothers can most definitely be

cruel. The feeble and old were once young and haughty. Age does not wipe away their infamous deeds."

The dwarf sighed and took another bite of his cheese. "Who made you their judge and executioner?"

"Who made you mine?" I countered, licking my lips just for show. "Your people, your clans are called 'dragon-slayers.' What is that but judge and executioner?"

"We're at a philosophical impasse, I see."

The air of the cave was noxious with my billowing smoke, and yet the dwarf only coughed once or twice, seeming to weather the gaseous cloud with little discomfort. He must have caught my look because he grinned mischievously.

"I've breathed the smoke of a hundred dragons," he said. "My lungs are as spotted and black as your heart, I'm afraid. A little more smoke won't kill me." His grin was interrupted by another cough, and then I understood.

"You are dying," I said. "Your work has slowly poisoned you."

"One might say the dragons slowly poisoned me, but yes, I take your meaning. Dangerous work, mine is. In more ways than one."

I wanted to laugh. The irony of it was delicious to my tongue. "Why not retire?" I asked. "Live out the paltry remainder of your days in peace."

He shook his grizzled head. "I do not know that word. Like you, I only know how to cleave and rend and snuff out life."

"Are you saying we're the same? Do not dare to presume. I am nothing like you, dragon-slayer. Imply it again and you will know neither peace nor war, only oblivion." My words were a warning, but my tired voice did not have much bite behind it. Slumber was encroaching on my eyelids, heavy with their old scales, and speaking became an effort.

"Shall I tell you a bedtime story, then?" the dwarf said. "I can see you want sleep."

"I do want it. My bones ache with it, but the time is not yet ripe. The sun has barely risen to noon."

"A little nap won't hurt."

"And let you bury your axe in my throat while I snore?"

"I promise I won't."

I laughed and it was thunder inside the cave's walls. "Your jest has enlivened me!" I widened my old eyes and shook the sleep from my lids.

"Well," said the dwarf, setting down his cheese and rubbing his fat fingers together, "let me tell you a story anyway. I have a few good ones in my hoard to share."

"Do you? And are they all about the death and destruction of my brethren?"

The dwarf looked sidelong and I could see my aim was true.

"Tell it then," I said. "Let me hear of your prowess. Let me know what master slayer now sits in my home and breathes my air as if it were his own. I want to hear of carnage, of the death your axe has wrought on the lords of the sky. Tell me. Tell me all your glories. You deserve to boast at your own wake. Tell me."

"It's not a boast," he said. "It's grim work, and I don't relish it. But in those days, I thought it necessary. For your brethren, as you call them, were killers. Lords of the sky? More like demons. So I was called to the wastelands to try and save the people who clung to life on those barren, smoking rocks."

I was barely listening now. Such tales were all the same. These common folk live hard lives, and we dragons only make them harder. If the dragon-slayer was looking for pity or absolution, he would not find it in my cave.

"I did not know the dragon's name at first," he continued. "Your folk guard those names like choicest treasure."

"We do," I said. "Most tongues are not fit to speak our names."

"And yet you told me yours."

"Have you spoken it yet?" I let a wreath of smoke trail from my nostril toward his head.

He coughed and batted it away uselessly. "Give me time. The dragon I tell of now was called Xirila. I learned her name from the charred grass that surrounded her nest atop a ruined keep."

"Charred grass? Is this a jest?"

"No. I have a way of listening. Since my birth, I've had such ways. Can't explain it. Just part of who I am."

"Intriguing." Though in truth, my lids were heavier than ever. Sleep was coming for me as surely as death.

"She was old. Older than you, I think."

"Is that so?" My lids were closing. I could feel the slick mucus of my eyes squeezing from the corners of my lids as they shut, and the sound of the dwarf's voice was muted in my ears. Only intermittently did I discern the words he spoke, such was my sleep coming upon me.

"Yes, she was old. So old, in fact, that the grass and rocks spoke of her as the mother of all dragons."

"There is no such mother," I mumbled, my tired jaws aching. "Those first primordial dragons were born from fire. From the very depths of the earth."

"Nevertheless, she was a mother."

He was silent for a moment, and my mind drifted through clouds of ancient smoke, through reeking fields of ash. My memory was long, but even I could not remember the moment of my birth. A dragon breaks out of his egg alone. There is no mother to comfort him, no mother to feed him his first taste of flesh. We must fly from our broken shells and find our own sustenance. Thus it was for me, for though I do not remember breaking forth from my shell, I remember that first taste of the air when I flew and the warmth of the hot, burning fields around the crag where I was born. That is all I remember. The air and the heat. And that first bite into the soft, juicy flesh of a boy shepherd, tending his flock on the far side of a distant mountain.

"And even though I knew she was a mother, I slew her," said the dwarf. "My axe smoked with the heat of her blood. She lay dying amongst the stones of the old keep, and in her death rattle, she spoke to me. Never had that happened before. Most dragons writhe around and bellow at the clouds, but they don't bother to speak to the bastard that carved up their bellies. This one spoke to me, and I think she was in some kind of stupor because what she said astounded me."

He paused again, I can only assume for dramatic effect. But his words mixed with my own faint dreams, for I was now as near to sleep as one can be without succumbing to full slumber. What I heard may have come from within my own head.

Take care of him, she said. My son.

"And did you?" I asked, barely awake. Sleep was my master now.

"No. It never crossed my mind."

That was a lie. I could hear it in the slight inhale of his breath. There's often an intake of breath when one speaks falsely, as if the lungs cannot bear to let too much air escape with the lies.

I was tumbling into a deep, dreamless slumber. I couldn't help it, but here I was, exposing myself to a dragon-slayer's axe. Careless in my old age.

He was spinning lies like a blanket to drowse me. No dragon mother cares for her son. No such words were spoken. But why, then, did he speak them? What net was he casting about?

I wanted to ask him, to catch him in his lies, but the words would not slip through my tired lips. I was too far gone. My eyes were shut, my breathing slowed to a wheezing hiss.

I was asleep. At his mercy. My day was finally spent.

———

THE CRUST WAS EVEN THICKER UPON MY EYES WHEN I awoke again.

"You did not kill me," I said, a mouth dry with old age and thirst.

"Aye, I did not." He was still close to me. I could hear the nearness of his voice.

"But you could have."

"Could I, now? Not so sure. You have a thick neck. Stiff and thick."

"Another insult."

"Just an observation."

I tried to open my eyes, but my lids did not have the strength. Sealed shut by the thick, yellow-gray mucus, harder than stones, which had leaked from my eyes in slumber, my eyes stayed locked in darkness. I could still smell the dragon-slayer, though, and his flesh made my mouth water.

"Hungry?" he said. "I'm right here for the picking."

"Indeed. But the plump fruit of your flesh carries with it a thorn."

The dwarf chuckled. "My axe is sharp, yes. But what's a small axe to your mighty jaws?"

"You want to die? Are you eager to be a dragon's meal?"

There was a long silence, and in that space, I tried again to open my eyes. The crust would not break.

"Not eager," he said at last, and nothing more.

He could surely see that my eyes were shut, but I didn't dare tell him that I could not open them. What time it was or how long I had slept, I did not know. I was at his mercy still, and still, he granted it to me.

"If not a dragon's meal, then why not a dragon's slayer?" I asked, putting the question to him.

"There's no rush. Let's hear another tale. This time from your mouth."

"You never finished yours," I said.

"Didn't I?"

"No."

"What is there to tell? She died, the mother dragon. Cursing me with her request."

"Cursing you?"

"Aye. I had trouble after that."

I pressed him. "What sort of trouble?"

"Trouble."

I could hear him sharpening his axe. My old bones felt like lead as I tried to move my neck and stretch. My jaws creaked like rickety wheels when I widened my mouth. The sharpening stopped.

"I never killed another dragon after that," he said. "Not for lack of trying, mind you. But something had changed. Her words were like a spell."

"I thought they never crossed your mind."

"They didn't. I'd forgotten them. But after many years, and many failures, I started thinking of them again. They sprang into my mind like a match struck in the darkness, and I started putting two and two together."

"And what did they equal?"

"That I had been cursed with a request I could never fulfill. I am a dragon-slayer. I swore a solemn oath to wipe out the scourge of your kind. How could I take care of a dragon-mother's son?"

"Scourge, am I? All dragons, then? I suppose the desire to slay us has nothing to do with our gold?"

The dwarf chuckled. A bitter sound. "Aye, the many villagers and townsfolk I've helped through the years were mighty glad to get hold of dragon gold. I was paid handsomely."

"I thought as much."

"But that's not why I took up my axe to hew the thick necks of wyrms."

"No?"

"The fire that burns hotter than a blacksmith's furnace is a scourge, gold or no gold. It's worth snuffing that deadly flame out no matter what payment is given."

"I am no forge. I am a living, breathing creature, same as you. I could say the same about your kind. Scourges all. Taking the mountains and the land from us, creeping into our caves and stealing our treasures. Bringing slayers to strike us dead because we should need food for our empty bellies."

"Is that your story? You've been wronged? All those poor folk down there who were burned by your flames deserved it?" He scoffed.

I made myself ready in case he did strike. My eyes could not see, but my other senses were alert. The dwarf was not the only one with a talent for listening. I could hear his heartbeat quicken, and the rising pitch of his voice. He was being roused.

"The last dragon I faced had done the same as you. Burnt every house and every villager. I watched from on high as he did it, weeping at the carnage and swearing an oath to exact justice."

"Vengeance."

"Justice. Flesh for flesh."

I didn't bother to correct him. Those villagers, whomever they were, were not innocent. I was sure of it. Corrupt, heartless, thieves, and worse. All humans and their related kin are such. After all, they swarmed the land eons ago and took it from its rightful masters. Us. The proto-wyrms and draconic overlords, my ancestors.

"You did not, however," I said, unable to keep the delicious smile from my lips, "exact your justice."

"No. I struck him while he slept, but my axe failed. The shaft broke as the iron hit the hard scales, and that first strike wasn't enough to fell him. He was roused. I barely escaped. Shame covered me like a cloak as I ran from those crags. I was as broken as my axe."

"But not so broken that you didn't find a new blade."

The dwarf chuckled as he nodded. "Aye. I'm not stupid. Anyone who parlays with a dragon had better come prepared."

"You came just to parlay, eh? To tell stories about the old days?"

"Not just stories."

"What then? To attempt a theft from my hoard? To strike me dead? That cannot be your aim, for you would have done it already."

"True. Can you not guess? I could have killed you while you slept. But I didn't. I could kill you now, with your eyes crusted shut. But I won't. What could be my purpose? What madness could have driven me here to talk with a dragon?"

"She was not my mother," I said.

The dwarf slid down from his perch upon my gold. I could hear the cascade of coins and precious metals clink as he descended. I could not see him, but I could hear his footsteps as they strode forward, right to my waiting jaws. I could snap him up in an instant, if I wanted.

But I didn't, and ever after, I wondered why.

"Would you like to see her grave?" he asked, and I could hear the sly smile behind the words.

If I had said nay, would the torture of never-knowing have eaten me up like rust consuming an ancient blade? I shall never know, because I did not reject his offer. Instead, I held my breath and thought of what it would be like to see the last remains of such a dragon, a draconic queen whom this dwarf claimed was older than I, a mother of dragons.

I breathed out, my ashen smoke filling the cave and choking the dragon-slayer. "Yes. Yes, I would like to see."

"Fly us there. I'll tell you the way."

But, of course, I could not see. My eyes were crusted shut. "And would you pick the yellowed mucus from my lids? Come close enough to tear the casing from my eyes?"

I heard him slide closer. I could not see, but I could feel the heat of his body and the disturbance in the air as he reached up with his hands.

Yes. Yes, he would reach up and remove my blindness. I had not thought it possible, but he was doing it. Peeling the crust from my eyes. The hardened mucus was stuck fast, and when he dug his fingers into to and ripped if off, it tore at my scales and stung with sharp pain. Of course, I did not cry out —no such satisfaction for him, if I could help it—but I'm sure my head shivered. And still he tore at the crust and flaked it away.

My lids were sensitive and sore, but when they were freed from their casing, I lifted them slowly so that blurry and reddened eyes could look upon the dragon-slayer again.

He stood close to my dry lips. He was staring up at me. Waiting.

"Climb upon my back and tell me the way to go," I said, disbelieving my own intentions. Were we really going to fly together, dragon and dragon-slayer? His axe was in his hand. Had he put it down to open my eyes? And had he now taken it up again? What fool was I! And yet I did not change course.

He pulled himself up onto my neck and fixed his position between the shoulder blades where my two wings sprouted. Perhaps he would lose his balance and plummet to certain death. I did not know, but I found myself hoping otherwise. At least until we found the grave. I told myself to fly steady, to keep him safe.

I crept to the cave's opening and took flight, my wings spreading like the mighty sails of human ships. Watery and blurred, my eyes could not tell what time of day it was. The sun was cold against my scales as I followed the directions the dragon-slayer gave me. He screamed them over the sound of the wind and my beating wings, and we traveled for a long time, even by dragon standards, across the valley and over the ring of mountains and even over the churning, dark sea that I knew bordered these lands.

As we traveled, I took to wondering. Would I find the bones of this old wyrm still intact beneath the earth? Should I even dare to look? A dragon's grave is not sacred, for we dragons have no true gods.

But it is private. Dragons are meant to die alone. We are all of us solitary creatures. That is why the dragon-slayer's blade is doubly cursed in our eyes. It does what it should not, and it sees what it should never see.

Would I be committing the same evil by looking upon the mound of this long-dead mother?

I flew on and pressed the doubts from my mind. I kept waiting for the dwarf to point out the spot, but he hardly spoke except to say, "Carry on," and so I did. For leagues, I flew. Across the known world. For such a distance and for so long that my wings began to tire, and every muscle in my old body ached. I said nothing to my cargo, but surely he could detect the quaver in my wings.

"It's not far," he said, in answer to my wordless struggles.

The old worries came back to me, that this was all a ruse, a feint to lull me into weakness so as to strike. But what could I do? I had made the foolish journey, and now I would find out the truth. I felt the unseen axe weigh upon me.

"This is the place," said the dragon-slayer.

"Yes," I said, almost against my will. "I feel it, a thing I cannot put into words."

"Look."

Below us, a little ways in the distance, there was a peak of blackened rock, plateaued into a flat plane, and upon that plane lay a pattern of white bones in the shape of dragon.

My mother.

No, not my mother. A dragon's mother does not care for her young. It was simply a dragon. A long-dead female of my kin.

"What's that?" said the dwarf, evident surprise in his voice.

I looked again. What had I missed? Were my eyes still too weak to see in this dim half-light of what might be day? The dwarf said he could hear things, but my ears could hear nothing.

The light from the clouded sky brightened for an instant, and I saw it. A thing, moving. A creature. A scavenger.

"Desecrator." The word hissed from my mouth.

The scavenger was moving over the white bones and picking at them, disturbing the perfect pattern of their form. A dragon's bones have power in them even after death. This thief was no doubt looking to steal such magic for itself, to harvest the greatness of this queen for its own paltry ends. It was always thus. These lesser beings tried to steal from their betters.

A fire burned in me hotter than I could contain.

"Careful," said the dwarf, "I think it's a lich."

"Even a lich may die by fire."

I opened my mouth, ready to unleash my red-hot wrath, but the dragon-slayer spoke again. "You'll destroy the bones," he said. "And what then?"

Yes, the bones. This grave of an ancient dragon-mother. It took all my effort, but I quenched the flame in my belly.

"Let us use claw and blade," I said in return.

"Careful."

I was not careful. I dove towards the scavenger, my teeth bared, my claws ready to strike. I did not see its knife, no doubt tipped in necrotic poison, nor did I bother to hear its hissing curse, but I felt the smoking blade scratch my scales as I swiped my claws across its billowing, ragged cloak. I caught nothing but cloak and air, but the lich caught my flesh, a small cut but the hot poison worked its way into my blood nonetheless. I roared, then felt my load lighten. The dwarf had jumped from my back and landed on the plateau beside the intruder. His axe was swinging, the lich cowering before it.

A spark of lightning flashed from the tussle between them, some spell no doubt, and the dwarf stumbled back. I saw the lich's face appear from beneath its hood, a pale, stricken face of death, and I lunged once more. This time my claws caught flesh, though it felt hollow beneath the skin when I dug my nails inside it. I lifted its skewered body toward my eyes so I could curse it, but the creature still contained some measure of power, and its eyes glowed red when I looked upon it, and I felt a spell usher from its mind, and the wound it gave me was deep. My heavy lids closed tight, but too late. I could feel my eyes burn beneath their sheaths.

I flung the lich into the gray sky. I did not care what happened to it, nor where it should go, I only wanted it away from this place, away from these sacred bones. My defense of them was absolute. I found myself ready to die for them. Something I had not expected.

When I pushed open my eyes again, I was exhausted. My body landed on the flat rock beside the dwarf. He was on his back, unmoving, the axe beside him, his hands empty. My weak vision couldn't be sure, but it seemed the dwarf's ruddy skin was burnt by unnatural fire. The lich's dark sorcery. He lay atop the bones of the dragon mother, and I could see now that the bones had sunken into the rock, becoming one with the mountain. The dwarf's body was like a scar running across that smooth flesh.

I nudged him with my snout, like a timid dog. He did not

stir. My eyes ached, and I felt the fire within me turn to sludge. I listened for the dwarf's breath, but my ears were weak, and I heard nothing. I could not see whether his chest rose or fell. Tired, I lay down beside him on the bones of the mother dragon. I took cold comfort in the fact that the thief had taken nothing of her remains.

Did I believe what the dwarf had said? Was this my mother? There was no frisson in my own bones, no affinity. I could sense the underlying power of these ancient bones, but nothing in the way of relation. Would I die here, so far from my own cave and all my treasures? Was this the dwarf's last revenge?

My innards felt like hardened stone. The blood was drying up within me. Both of us would die here, it seemed.

"Is the creature gone?" The dwarf's voice was weak. I confess, I thought he'd expired, but my eyes dimly caught his body shift and stand. He reached down and picked up his axe.

"Do not waste your strength," I wheezed. "I am dying."

"I can see that. But at least you're here. A fitting end, to die upon your mother's grave."

"I shall not die upon these bones. Power is in them, yes, but I feel no closeness to their marrow. We dragons do not know our mothers."

The dwarf turned away and looked into the blackening clouds. "I thought, perhaps..."

"I told you."

"Yes, but I thought, well, we all have mothers. She had told me..."

"Dragons lie."

"Did she think I would spare her?" His voice was labored, each word a cracked breath.

"There is nothing for us here," I answered.

He was silent for a long time. My eyes were burning and weak; I could barely make out his shape in the gloom.

"Can you fly?" he said.

"If you guide me." I wanted to lie down in my cave, to feel the chink of gold pieces on my smooth belly again.

The dwarf nodded, but I saw his body twitch and his face wince. He was not much better than I.

Our flight felt longer on the return journey. My wings were heavier than lead, and my eyesight grew worse in the darkness. Without the dwarf's help, I would not have made it home. My body would have crashed into some cliffside or kept sailing into oblivion, my wings giving out their strength, all of me crashing to the depths of the earth.

Instead, we found my cave and the familiar gleam of my treasures. I was nearly spent.

"You have come to kill me," I said with labored breaths. "I was foolish to think otherwise."

The dwarf was silent for a long time. I wondered if he had fallen asleep, or if the lich's wound had stymied him.

"In the morning," I continued. "Give me one last night to prepare."

All was silent after that. I could not even be sure if he dismounted from my back. My slumber was so deep that I thought my body had sunk below the piles of gold and jewels and fell into the very depths of the rock itself, bone and mountain melded into one.

When I awoke, my eyes would not open. But I knew it

was morning. I smelled the morning air, and the dew. I smelled dead flesh too.

The dwarf had fallen off my back. His body lay beside my own, but while mine still throbbed with some measure of life, his was now deep in the hallways of death.

"That was not my mother," I muttered to myself in the dark. "Why did he bring me there?"

In the silence of my cave, I could find no answers. I remembered what he'd said. What the dragon mother had said.

Take care of him.

But she was false. And so was this dwarf. I was not taken care of. No dragon ever is. We are born alone and die alone, unless a dragon-slayer should kill us.

I could feel my innards growing cold with every haggard breath. I could no longer see the sun. The crust on my eyes was too thick, and there was no one left to clean them. What can a blind dragon hunt? What can a dragon do without its fire?

I shifted my body slightly and brushed up against the corpse of the dwarf. He must have died just before the dawn, for his body was still fleshy and not yet hardened by death. I knew what I must do, but the thought made me sicken, and I cursed myself for such cravenness. Perhaps it was good that my fire had died. The lich's curse had made manifest the already-spreading cancer of my weakness.

I sniffed the body, and though death was apparent, there was still his familiar smell. Why did I hesitate? Why did I resist? Hunting was now an impossible feat. The only thing which could satiate the last of my hungers was evident, but still, I could not do it. The ease of opportunity did not overcome my revulsion.

What a revenge he has had upon me! His body and mine should die together, our flesh rotting and our bones intermingling with my treasures. The thought sickened me. My jaws ached, my stomach gnawed at me, and yet I could not bring myself to devour my enemy.

Movement at the opening of my cave made me stiffen. Because I was cold rock now, it was easy to play dead. I waited and listened.

A thief. Scavenger.

I thought of the lich, but this was not that sorcerous undead. This was a human being: living, breathing, greedy. The human slinked into my abode, careful not to disturb my jewels and coins, but I could sense its covetousness, its desire. I had once felt such desires, but now I was too tired. I was ravenous with hunger, but would this human walk openly into my jaws?

He stepped over my gold and knelt before the body of the dwarf. What game was he playing at? I heard him pry something from the dwarf's grip. The axe.

All these treasures, and what he wanted was a piece of sharp iron? I almost laughed at the absurdity of it. Was he going to kill me, then? I knew from the moment he arrived, and I could smell his stench, that this human was no dragon-slayer. And yet would he do what the dwarf had not? It was too much. An insult. Something inside me roused to old anger. The hinges of my jaws loosened, and without warning, I struck. He dropped the axe when my teeth bit.

His flesh was stale in my mouth, his bones weak. As I

crunched and swallowed, I knew the taste. Famine. Encroaching death. Perhaps starvation was sweeping the land.

The paltry meal was not enough, and now that my belly had been given a morsel, it wanted more. The dwarf was not so dead that he was rotting, and even so, I had eaten rotten meat before.

And yet.

Words rang in my ears, the dying words of a mother. And they were a curse.

My eyes would not open. The darkness of the world was complete. And the fire which burns hotter than the smith's furnace had grown cold.

Soon there would be two dead things in the cave of the dragon. A scourge and slayer. A dragon and a dwarf. And who would remember us but the dust and the gold?

SAD CAVERN

Drys-Gul was a gloom wizard.

What *is* a gloom wizard? This is the wrong question. To define a gloom wizard is only incidental. What a gloom wizard *does* is of much more consequence.

A gloom wizard does not practice some obscure form of sorcery; he (or she) is often an ordinary wizard to start, with typical training and typical powers. But the gloom wizard is not typical in all things. No, he (or she) is overcome with an unearthly, unwieldy spirit of melancholy. The anguish, despair, and unrelenting sadness of the person is such that a mystic sort of gloominess descends upon them, imbuing them with a supernatural, almost god-like state of melancholia, and it is this power which transforms the ordinary wizard into the gloom wizard.

After a time, this anguished state results in the dissolving of the human form into some other physical manifestation: a gnarled tree, a decrepit castle, a sulfur-breathing cave.

———

"Go on, Gilfore," said Tark, "go in. Or let me lead if you're too cowardly."

Gilfore shivered but he wouldn't let the dwarf take the first position; such a thing would give Tark the upper hand and Gilfore would never hear the end of it. But still, the bard didn't move. He hesitated on the threshold of the cavern and felt his stomach sink as he gazed upon the hideous face carved into the side of the mountain: its gaping jaws formed the entranceway to hidden tunnels below. The face was troll-like—ugly and sad and misshapen—and it made Gilfore wonder if such a path was really necessary. He also wondered who had carved this face around the cave opening. If they didn't go through the cave into the mountains, they'd have to go over the mountains and that seemed even less desirable in Gilfore's estimation. Journeys over mountains rarely go well. The bard's hesitation was shattered, however, by the clamor of rough voices coming over the ridge behind them.

"Go on, you bastard!" cried Tark, shoving a mailed fist at Gilfore. "Before they shoot us!"

A scout had spotted Tark and the others and shouted to his comrades climbing up the opposite side of the hill.

Anya couldn't make out the exact words, but she could hear the urgency in the scout's voice. Soon the valley where she and her companions stood would be swarming with Lord Brecken's men. And a flurry of their arrows would follow. She looked at the leather bag in her hand and wondered if it might not be better to fling the gold pieces back towards the soldiers. Maybe then she and the others might live.

Gilfore practically dove into the mouth of the cavern, Tark on his heels. Anya ran in too, banishing thoughts of giving up the gold; she knew in her gut what surrender would mean. Alum the druid came last, chanting under his breath and moving quicker than Anya would've expected. *Perhaps,* she thought, *I shouldn't judge a man based on his baldness and round belly.*

The cavern of Drys-Gul welcomed them in, its forlorn jaws unmoved by their haste or panic. It was glad of their company, that was all. A foul belch of sulfurous air streamed forth from the cave, but none of the thieves minded. They'd rather gag on noxious gas than on the hangman's noose.

Once the last strands of Alum's tattered robes had passed the mouth of the cave, the voices of Lord Brecken's men ceased. Light filtered in from outside, but there was a shimmer of translucent mist that hung down over the cave mouth, closing off the outer world. No one saw how the mist appeared, but it was there, a veil between the sunlit outside world and the damp interior of the cavern. Anya wasn't sure how, but she knew that nothing could pass through that mist, neither Brecken's men nor her own companions. No more coming in, no more going back. Despite its shimmering, crystalline appearance, the veil of mist was no trifle. It was a trap for any who dared pass through. And after all, wasn't this why the companions had chosen such a way? Weren't they all too-happy to let the enchantments of Drys-Gul shield them?

"This sunlight won't last us forever," grumbled Tark. "Who brought the torches for you upworlders?"

Gilfore looked insulted. "I told you to pack them. Now it's suddenly my fault you don't have any?"

The dwarf growled at the bard, but Alum stepped nimbly between them. "No one is blaming you, dear Gilfore," said the holy man.

"But no one has any torches," sneered Tark. "It's not much to me, but you humans can't see past your toes in the underdark."

Gilfore's eyes flashed even in the looming darkness. "And whose fault is it—"

But Alum held up a hand again. "My holy symbol will lend us light." He took it from under his robes and lifted the chain from around his neck. The pendant was nothing more than a huge egg-shaped bronze-colored stone, but it glimmered in the half-light, and when Alum held it aloft and uttered a prayer to his god, the egg glowed like a fat wax candle.

Anya wondered what the holy man worshiped, but she couldn't recall any stories her brother had told her about Alum's deity. *What sort of god has an egg for a holy symbol?* she thought.

In the light they could see that the tunnel was huge. The ceiling was high above and covered in stalactites—white as bone—while the ground was peppered with gleaming white stalagmites, and the width was even wider than the yawning jaws of the cavern's mouth. What surprised them most of all was the color of the cave-rock. Veined with streaks of crimson and indigo, the walls and ceiling were the color of pink flesh; if the rogues hadn't known the cave was made of rock they would've thought they were caught in the maw of some beast: a lion, or wolf, or dragon.

Alum's holy egg shined forth to reveal where the massive tunnel went: down into looming blackness.

"Blades a'ready," commanded Tark. He was least bothered by the approaching descent; a dwarf relished the coldness and dim light beneath the earth.

Gilfore, however, shivered. "Oh, how I wish I'd worn a thicker cloak! These damp dungeons always leave my bones aching!"

"Quit yer crying!" snarled Tark. "You'd complain of your old bones aching even in a bed with two buxom whores."

"Oh, hush! We can't all be earthworms like you!" sneered the bard.

Anya thought Tark was going to bury his hand-axe in Gilfore's skull, but then Alum shushed them.

"Do you hear?" he said. His eyes were wide and white, glistening in the egg-light.

They all stopped breathing for a split second and listened. Faint and clear came the ringing notes of a harp. Gilfore smiled and straightened his shoulders.

"Exeter's Reel," he said knowingly. "Well-played too. Takes nimble fingers to do the bridge."

"Who the hell cares what it's called!" hissed Tark. "I want to know who's playing it."

"And whether we have to worry," added Alum.

Anya kept quiet. She squeezed the bag of gold tighter and kept her other mailed fist hovering over the pommel of her brother's sword. It was still sheathed, but she was reconsidering whether to unleash the naked blade. The brightness of the harp's notes seemed unnatural and sinister as they wafted up from the dark tunnel ahead.

Gilfore took his lead position more cheerfully, though, unperturbed by the music. He was almost giddy about it. And in fact, there was no need of worry. When they descended the narrow stone stairs, they found themselves in a small but high-ceilinged little cave, and in the center of the cave floated the source of the astonishing music.

The harp was playing itself.

No fingers plucked its strings; no hands caressed its frame. It floated in midair like a golden cloud.

"Magic," said Tark, his voice tinged with the contempt that all dwarfs have for arcane powers.

"Someone has placed an enchantment upon it," pronounced Gilfore, matter-of-factly. "The question is, where is our master magician now?"

Anya didn't speak up to contradict. It was possible that a magician had enchanted the harp, but it was also possible that the harp was intrinsically magical, that it had been created by magic wood from a mystical forest or strung with threads of immortal horse hair. Or perhaps the cave itself had brought about the enchantment. No doubt Gilfore had assumed the most likely course of events, and for that reason, Anya saw no need to argue. But still, she wondered.

"It's a trap, whoever set it," said Tark. "Leave it be and we'll yet live."

"Leave it be?" Gilfore was shocked. "How could you be so short-sighted? A magic harp that plays itself? Why, I could make mountains of coin out of this! What demand there'll be for Gilfore and his magic harp!"

"Watch yourself, Gil," said Alum. "Tark may be right about a trap."

"Then use your godly vision, dear druid. Do you see the astral shiver of a trap or no?"

Alum held his glowing egg in front of his face, so closely in fact, that all he could physically see were the bright beams and stars that burst forth from the light itself. But beyond the physical, within the plane of insubstantial spirit, he could see with total clarity: the astral realm as it coexisted with the corporeal.

"No traps. As far as I can tell," Alum said, lowering his holy symbol and looking dazed from the light.

"More arcana," grumbled Tark. "I don't trust it, or you, or you stupid egg." He scowled at the druid, then turned to the bard. "Touch that thing if you want, but I'm leaving you to your fate."

The dwarf turned and thudded his way back up the narrow stairs. Anya almost followed him—prudence would dictate it—but she didn't want to abandon the bard either. It was cold in this high-ceilinged chamber, and forlorn, as if no one had ever stopped to hear the music before, as if the harp had been playing for centuries, for no one.

"Trap or no trap, I think you'd better leave it alone," said Alum, also turning to go. "What if it won't stop playing? When we reach the other side of this cave and emerge into sunlight again, there'll be no use hiding from Brecken's men if that racket is trilling all the time." He disappeared through the narrow gap above, right after Tark. Gilfore almost opened his mouth to protest the word "racket," but instead he silently vowed to never share his future riches with either the dwarf or the druid. He alone would benefit from the enchanted harp's powers.

Only Anya remained with the bard, and she—as was her wont—said nothing.

Gilfore's hand trembled as he reached for the harp. Now that he had come to it, fear gripped him. But the bell-like ringing of the strings was so sweet, and the melody so effortless and swift, that at last the bard conquered his inner cowardice and took the harp into his hands.

At once, the music stopped.

Anya and Gilfore both looked at each other, eyes wide. They waited, but in the breath-holding silence nothing happened.

"I hope..." Gilfore's voice caught in his throat. "I hope I didn't break it," he said. He looked at Anya again as if he were apologizing to her and waited to receive absolution.

Anya thought it entirely possible that Gilfore had broken it, but she didn't say anything. She didn't want to add to his woe.

———

I WELCOME YOU, TRAVELERS, EVEN AS I KNOW YOU HAVE come to meet your doom. Step into the depths of my jaws. Breathe the reeking stench of the mountain's belly. Come, foolhardy ones! Find the freedom you seek! Join in my gloom!

When Anya woke up, she heard the faint sounds of the voice echo through her head, fading away eventually into the silence of the cave. The others were asleep. Gilfore had his magic harp enfolded in his arms, hugging it like a newborn kitten.

The tunnel where they slept was chilly, but the group refused to huddle together for warmth. Anya's thin burlap blanket did little to stave off the cold. And Alum's glowing egg—though it illuminated the pitch-blackness of the caves—did nothing to provide heat. Right now the holy symbol shimmered faintly in the darkness; the druid had turned its radiance down so that they could get some rest without needing to be blinded by the utter lack of light. Of course, Tark would've preferred no light, but the humans insisted—especially Gilfore, who feared an ambush. In order to sleep, Anya had taken off her helmet but not her armor. She put her helmet back on now. The others still hadn't seen her face; she had made sure to remove her helm once she could hear three noses snoring. Now that she had awoken, her mask would resume its post.

Why are you hiding? They know that you are not your brother. They know that Alaric is dead. Anya heard her own voice repeat these things, but in echo to all her thoughts came another: *Do they? Do they really know?*

Alum's holy symbol made faint shadows on the walls. Those shadows flickered and danced, even though the light of the egg was constant. Anya thought such movements of light and shade were odd. Then the shadows grew bigger, and the light grew brighter and more colorful. Hues of red and green and blue began to dance with the egg's light, and that light—a faint, sickly yellow—was mixing suddenly with a richer, deeper, more golden glow that came from further down the tunnel. All of the flickering colors, in fact, had their origin from around that curve, from the direction the group had yet to travel. The colors of light danced like tongues of flame, calling to the travelers. And the shadows on the walls transformed into fiendish shapes, devils and ghouls and slithering wyrms. Anya reached a hand and touched the rock wall; her palm blocked out the shadow-ghoul dancing there, turning it back into solid darkness.

She turned to wake the others only to find Tark sitting up, eyes wide open.

"I should've smell it," he said. "Treasure." His beady eyes gleamed in the colorful light. When he stood up and scurried toward the golden glow, Anya was surprised that neither the druid nor the bard awoke. Tark's movements were hardly stealthy; he banged about like a hungry pig. But the other two snored contentedly, while Tark was already around the bend of the tunnel, heading towards the colorful lights. He hadn't invited Anya to follow.

She was more careful when she moved. Creeping along the narrow passageway, she did her best to keep a distance from the dwarf. But all her caution was for nothing. For when she found the cave with the treasure, she might as well have been invisible. Tark paid her no heed; he only had eyes for the gold and gems.

And what gold and gems they were. Coins of bright gold were gathered in heaping piles, while rubies and emeralds dotted the golden landscape, like shiny drops of blood and liquid blades of grass. Fashioned in twisted, serpentine shapes, the gems almost resembled crafted glass, as if some master glassblower had devised them. But they were solid and heavy, true gemstones and not heated sand.

All the treasure sparkled in the red-gold and blue-green and amethyst flames of magic torchlight. For ensconced around the huge chamber were torches upon torches of enchanted flame, all in different colors, making compliment to the colors of the gold and gems. It was a kaleidoscope room, a swirling rainbow that made everything seem off-kilter, as if one's head were drunk on strong wine. It was hard to see exactly where the treasure ended and the torchlight began.

Tark exhaled an awestruck sigh. Anya could see that his body shivered with anticipation and desire. She almost said something, almost tried to warn him. There was some danger here, she could feel it, traces of the voice in her head whispering, *Step into the depths of my jaws... Come, foolhardy ones!* That voice which was both invitation and doom.

But Anya said nothing. She watched as Tark stooped over the heaps of gold and jewels and took a handful into his grasp. She watched as he shoved mailed fist after mailed fist into the piles and stuffed what treasures he could into his pockets and knapsack. He gathered the treasure with a gluttonous appetite that Anya knew would never fully be sated.

But then Tark stopped. His pockets and bag bulged with treasure. He sighed again, but this time the sigh was one of contentment, of fullness. He was done.

When he turned around and saw Anya watching him, he smiled. He saw her, but he seemed to look through her at the same time. There was something delirious about his smile. Anya waited for him to speak, but Tark said nothing, sweeping past her and going back down the narrow passageway to rejoin the others. If there was any doom placed on the treasure, it hadn't revealed itself yet. Tark was practically skipping along as he passed by her.

Perhaps Anya's intuition was wrong. Perhaps this treasure was simple a treasure: a king's ransom in gold and jewels, the chance for Anya herself to retire into luxury, a lucky stroke that would set her up for life. The paltry coins they stole from Lord Bracken would be nothing compared to even a few handfuls of these gold pieces.

She realized suddenly that she wasn't holding the coin bag that had been stolen from Bracken. Of course she had put it down to get some sleep. Creeping along as carefully as possible, she went back into the chamber where Gilfore and Alum were sleeping. When she saw Tark, he was sitting off by himself, cooing over his new-found gems.

He paid her no mind. Anya searched the ground for the leather bag, but her stomach clenched as she saw that there was no sign of it. She had been carrying it before they stopped to rest... or had she? Suddenly Anya realized that she couldn't remember the last time she had seen or felt the coin bag. She knew that she'd carried it into the entrance, under the mouth of Drys-Gul. She could remembered that much. But after Gil found the harp, after they'd walked for hours, after bedding down when their feet could hardly move another step... She couldn't remember.

And now it was gone.

But Tark didn't even notice her frantic searching; he had found a more precious cargo. And Gil hugged his harp like a baby. Alum might forgive her; perhaps his god was merciful. Anya decided she would say nothing; let them think what they would. If they asked about the coins or wondered where the bag had gone, then she would feign surprise. Perhaps they would believe her...

————

GILFORE'S HIS FINGERS SEEMED NOT HIS OWN. THEY were a blur of movement across the harp, and the tune was both light and melancholy, a happy sadness that carried with it the air of something fey. Even as the song crescendoed into a rousing climax, there was a lilt to it that echoed another tune, a distant melody that was never-ending, that was eternal, filled with both joy and darkness. Gilfore saw nothing else but the strings, heard nothing else but the song, felt nothing else but the rapture and ecstasy of creation. Anya and the others were silent, caught up in the rolling and swelling and ringing of notes, as if caught in a rising tide or a swift river. Where they were headed, they did not care, so long as Gilfore kept playing.

Anya wasn't sure how long they sat and listened to the bard. After a time the song ceased, but when it ended or how or what the last notes were, none of them could say. Eventually they realized that the tunnel was silent and that Gilfore's fingers had stopped.

"What happened?" asked Alum. "Won't you keep playing?"

The bard didn't answer at first. He stared at his feet, unmoving. His fingers were poised just next to the harp strings, but they quivered slightly as they hung in midair, unable or unwilling to pluck another note. Gilfore acted as if he were alone, as if no one or nothing existed apart from himself.

"Finally some quiet," mumbled Tark. He hadn't really been listening to the music. The rubies in his palm were all the beauty he needed, and he continued to gaze longingly at them.

But Gilfore didn't even reply to the dwarf's jab. He didn't move. His fingers still lingered near the strings, frozen as if by some enchantment.

"That was the best music you have ever played, my friend," said Alum, still jolly. He hummed a few notes of Gil's now-faded tune. "Absolutely the best."

Anya stepped toward Gil. For a split second she considered the wisdom of what she intended, but wisdom was not always wisdom: sometimes it was undue caution. Self-preservation. Saving her own skin wasn't always the answer, she reminded herself. So she reached out and put a hand on Gilfore's shoulder. What she feared, she couldn't say, but she overcame that fear to help her companion.

"Gil," she said softly, only to him.

The bard blinked, and Anya could feel his muscles move and his breath inhale slightly.

"Gil," she continued, "are you finished?" She kept her voice low so that the others couldn't hear the pitch of her voice, the feminine qualities. She wondered, with a bit of panic, whether Alaric would be so gentle.

Her words did something to Gilfore. His fingers lost their frozen tension; they laid themselves down on the bard's lap. His head hung low now, spent of all energy or desire.

Methodically, trance-like, he took the harp from his lap and strung it over his shoulder and across his back.

"I hope we shall have the pleasure of hearing you play again," said Alum, cheerfully. "And what a pleasure! Most delightful! I'd say that new harp suits you."

But Gilfore seemed not to hear him, nor to recognize any of the companions.

"What was that tune, I wonder?" said the druid. "Like nothing I've ever heard! It was quite marvelous, Gil. I shouldn't wonder that you won't starve again if you can play music like that!"

But Gilfore said nothing.

Anya searched his face, hoping to find some sign of what had happened.

But the bard's face was blank, unmoved. When words finally escaped his lips, they seemed to come from another mouth. "It's no use," he whispered. "It's gone."

"What's gone?" said Anya. She was frightened of this strange, abrupt shift in the bard.

Gilfore didn't look at her; he didn't even seem to be speaking to her. "The joy," he said. "The joy." And he sighed. He stood up and started walking back down the tunnel. The others followed, but whether they realized it or not, they kept a distance between themselves and the bard.

From that moment on, he never touched the harp again.

———

It was becoming harder and harder to get Tark to move. He stopped often and suddenly, always reaching into his pockets and taking out a few gems. Then he would fondle them, gaze at their beauty, and delight in their gleaming colors. Gilfore usually said nothing, but Alum would plead with the dwarf.

"I am not one to urge haste without reason, Tark," the druid would say. "But provisions are growing dangerously short, and we cannot eat gems and jewels."

Food, drink, or otherwise did not entice Tark. His sustenance was provided by the riches of the treasure.

Anya was also worried about their rations, but she grew more worried about what strange powers seemed at work. Gilfore still said nothing; he never touched the magic harp nor made any attempt at interaction with the others. He was walking as if half-alive, overcome with some melancholy of spirit that Anya feared would cost them all dearly if not remedied. Tark, on the other hand, was gripped by a kind of mania. When he talked, he talked of nothing else, and he spoke in excited whispers—not to his companions—but to his new-found gold. He babbled about the power and prestige that awaited him, about his future as a dwarf-lord, rich in majesty and wealth. He thanked the gems for coming into his possession.

Alum huffed and fretted under his breath. "What are we to do? What are we to do?" he said, looking desperately to Anya for some aid.

Anya didn't even shrug. What could they do but continue through the caverns and try to drag Tark along?

After an hour of walking in fits and starts, urging an ever-distracted Tark to keep moving, Alum began to mumble a prayerful chant. He turned the egg-shaped symbol in his hand as he prayed, making sure to keep it aloft for them to still see by its light.

At first the druid prayed softly, but then Anya thought she heard his indistinct mumbling receive an answer: a loud buzzing came from further up the tunnel. Alum heard it too, and his face perked up, eyes alight. He chanted louder, and pushed ahead of the morose Gilfore and shuffling, giddy Tark. Anya wasn't sure whether to follow on his heels or hang back. Something possessed her to put a hand out to feel the cave wall of the tunnel. With shock, she pulled her hand quickly away from the surface. It wasn't cold stone or even wet dirt. The walls of the tunnel felt coarse, like shredded paper pasted together in uneven layers.

Like a wasps' nest, she thought.

Now she did push ahead of the others and went after the druid. The tunnel narrowed and rounded out into a small, circular opening that shone with the same bright yellow of Alum's egg, only more intense. Anya had to duck to go through, and she wondered how Alum had even squeezed his round belly into such a hole. The chanting of the druid was full-throated now, matched by at least two dozen other chanting voices. When Anya emerged into this new cave, her breath caught in her throat.

Alum was there, standing in the center of the room, head bowed, chanting loudly. All around him swirled his fellow devotees. They flew on razor-sharp, translucent wings, which held aloft their two-sectioned black and yellow bodies. The feelers on their heads twitched up and down, back and forth, snaking about in a kind of dance, while their six spindly legs played like fiddles in mid-air, issuing forth a harsh buzzing sound that resembled Alum's chant, but which was more alien, more primordial than his human voice could imitate. Alum was in the midst of his fellow acolytes now, all of their chanting and buzzing turning into a deafening prayer.

Wasps, Anya thought in horror. She saw their stingers, long and black and razor-sharp. She wanted to back away, dive down through the small opening and return to Tark and Gilfore. But Alum was transfixed, standing at the center of this swarm of insects. His eyes saw only the object in the center of the cave.

All them—druid and giant wasps—surrounded in worship their glowing idol. Hanging from the ceiling of the cave was a conical object, fat on the bottom and tapering to a smaller, more pointed top. It looked fairly smooth, but now that Anya looked closely, she could see that it was actually layers upon layers of paper and mud which had been fashioned together to form a solid mass. And yet it glowed from within: a deep golden yellow that resembled sunlight and amber.

Anya saw clearly now. Alum's holy symbol had not been an egg at all. It had been a nest. A giant, glowing, golden wasps' nest. Whether Alum worshipped the nest itself or whatever lived inside of it, Anya did not know, and she feared to find out.

The nest hung from a kind of branch, one that was thick and knotted and covered with tiny hair-like strands. But it was not the branch of a tree; it was a strong root in a vast network of roots, all of them protruding from the earthen ceiling above. To Anya it looked as if they were under the ground where a massive tree had dug its home, and these were the roots of its ancient life. The roots snaked in and out of the wet dirt above, forming a labyrinth of intertwined, gnarled limbs. And hanging from the longest and thickest limb was the glowing wasps' nest, the druid's idol.

Alum dared to approach the nest, his own glowing imitation of it still held high in his hand. As he approached, he bowed and chanted all the more loudly, coming in supplication to his god. The wasps swarmed around him. Alum raised his arms, letting the holy symbol in his hand fall with a clatter to the ground. He took the great nest into his upraised palms, enfolded it into his arms, and with a violent tug, wrenched it from the root on which it hung. The wasps swarmed and soared throughout the chamber, encircling the druid and the god-nest he now held against his chest. When Alum turned toward Anya, his eyes looked past her, caught up in zealous ecstasy, consumed by a divine trance. He continued to chant in that buzzing, inhuman way, as if he had swallowed a mouthful of the wasps and they now lived within him, a discordant chorus plucking the strings of his vocal cords.

The tree roots above them shook, disturbed by the severing of nest from branch. Then the wasps deserted the druid, flying back toward the roots and the damp earth above them, digging themselves into unseen holes in the flesh of the underworld.

Alum paid no mind. He cradled his idol in his arms and departed.

———

ALARIC HAD BEEN GIDDY THE DAY ANYA TOOK HIS armor. He had lain in the grass, struck by some vivid pattern in the clouds, and Anya watched him from a little ways off.

This will mean he can keep on laughing at the clouds, she had thought as she creeped toward his breastplate, helmet, gauntlets, and sword. She watched his face contort into shapes that Anya had never seen on her brother before. His laughter—his giggles and smiles—they were upsetting to witness. He seemed possessed of a demon or put under some heinous spell. All Anya could think was, *Why is he watching the clouds? Why is he laughing?*

But the laughter soon died. Anya remembered that. The laughter gave in to a terrible silence. And when Anya went over to take his inheritance, she never feared his wrath. Her brother was lost, caught in some terrible void, unable to see or to hear or to feel.

Anya put the armor on and girded the sword as Alaric lay in the grass and stared at nothing. She put the helmet over her head while her brother never moved. She even spoke a word to him—*What was it? I can't remember now*—but Alaric never answered. She walked away down the hill, the tall grass waving against her legs, the broadsword heavy on her hips.

What did the others say when I told them about Alaric? Anya couldn't seem to recall. *Did I say anything?* she wondered. But they had accepted her, they had let her slay that one guard and take the gold from the caravan. All of that mayhem felt like a dream now, now that Anya wandered the cavern of Drys-Gul and had trouble remembering her brother's face. *If I take off this helmet,* she wondered, *what face will I see?*

But there were no mirrors in the cavern, nor even pools of water in which to gaze. There was nothing but darkness and the strange light that emanated from Alum's idol. The wasps' nest glowed brighter than the miniature holy symbol had, but it didn't matter much.

There was nothing to see in the cavern except the dark stone walls.

And her companions were utterly silent.

———

Do you know the place to which you have come? Do you know where it is you stand, alone and in such silence?

Anya didn't dare take the wasps' nest from Alum, but its light was enough to help her see. The walls of the tunnel were no longer stone or rock. They were soft and rubbery to touch, their surface more like a series of bulbous tubes intertwined together in a vast network of tendrils or ropes than like any kind of geological formation. When Anya ran her fingers down the surface, the fleshy surface quivered.

She turned to her companions and saw them all sitting on the ground. None of them moved. She realized now that they would never move.

Panic finally burst through the lid Anya had been keeping on it. She had known for a long while that these caverns were overlaid with some curse, with some kind of magic that was enchanting the party, but had wanted to deny it, like bad news a person refuses to face. But she could no longer refuse. The dread had come and she could not suppress it.

The panic and the dread mixed with a terrible question that wouldn't leave her: *Why not me? Why have I not succumbed to these curses?*

Anya took off her helmet. She needed her companions to see her face. She needed to have someone see her face.

When she looked again at the cavern, the walls were solid limestone, veined with greens and browns and blues. She quickly ran her fingers along the surface.

Hard and cold.

She felt her face. There was no conscious explanation why, but she knew she needed to feel the skin, to recognize the contours of her bones. The feeling of her own face surprised her.

What was I expecting? she thought. *Nothing has changed.*

But everything had.

———

"Play something, Gil." Anya's voice cracked. The fear she felt was rising to choke her. She no longer cared that they could all hear her. "Tark!" she continued, turning toward the dwarf. "Look at these gems!" She picked them up from the ground where Tark had let them fall. "I've never seen anything so beautiful! You will be the richest dwarf in Veshi with treasures like these!"

But Tark sat like a gnarled stump on the damp floor of the cave. The gold coins and serpent-shaped rubies spilled out of his pockets and knapsack, littering the cold dirt around him.

"Pick them up!" Anya found herself shouting. She tried

shoving the gemstones into Tark's hands, but his fingers were limp, and the stones fell with a soft clatter.

When Anya turned to the druid, he was laying on his back. Too stiff to be asleep or resting, he lay like a man pinned to the ground, arms outstretched, legs taut. Anya bent down and shook him. But Alum's eyes were not closed; he was not unconscious, nor asleep. He was done. Defeated. The bronze idol of his bird-god was laying in the dirt as well, an inch away from his outstretched hand. But Alum didn't even notice. When Anya tried to put it back in his hand, his fingers didn't move, and the idol flopped out, rolling onto the dirt with a thud.

Anya looked around: all three men were unresponsive, their faces blank, their eyes distant. None of them moved or spoke or reacted to anything in their surroundings. It was as if the world, the cavern, Anya herself had ceased to exist. And the things that had brought them such pleasure and ecstasy— the harp, the treasure, the idol—were as nothing now: refuse and junk to be abandoned in the dirt.

The fear had reached her mouth, and Anya couldn't speak. Next, the fear would rise to her cheeks and make them burn, and then to her eyes and tears would begin to fall. Desperate thoughts filled her head.

Should I leave them? I can take these things for myself, sell the harp and the idol, use the trove of gems and gold to live a queen's life. All these things will certainly make up for the bag of gold I lost. I can even bribe Bracken, repay him what was stolen and still have a king's ransom to live on myself.

They'll never know. Gilfore, Tark, and Alum, they won't

ever know. They will rot here if I leave them. But they'll never know.

The voice in her head was calm, rational.

They have found the gloom, haven't they?

The voice in her head was not her own.

Just like Alaric.

"But why not me!" Anya felt the words coming out of her mouth in a desperate flood she could not contain. "Why have I been spared? What makes me different from the others?"

She looked briefly at Gilfore, Tark, and Alum, hoping that her outburst would shake them from their stupor, but she wasn't surprised to see that they made no movements, gave no reactions.

Trees that never bud or bloom, dead as driftwood, but never-dying. That is the power of the gloom wizard.

Anya shivered at the words, though she didn't know why. She had no recollection of ever hearing about a gloom wizard.

"Who's there?" she demanded, her voice cracking under her own fear. "What are you?"

The stone walls around her changed again: they were like bark from a dead tree, and carved in the bark were gnarled faces, scowling and sad.

What are you?

"I am Anya the tanner's daughter!" She said it fiercely. She wanted the voice, the presence that invaded her mind to know that she was defiant, that she would not give in.

Why have you come?

The defiance was gone. Anya was deflated, like a waterskin that had been stepped on and burst. She didn't know why she'd come. Or she didn't care to know.

Somewhere in the recesses of her mind she knew there must have been a reason to take her brother's armor, a reason to fall in with his old companions, a reason to steal Lord Bracken's gold.

But she no longer had the gold. The bag had disappeared. *Or did I ever have it?* she wondered. But that thought was only a passing fancy, a mad thought that bore no semblance to reason or sanity. *Of course I had the bag of gold. Of course.*

Why have you come?

I don't know, Anya thought. *I can't say.*

Won't.

Anya wouldn't let the voice inside her win. There must have been a reason. Anya *knew* there must have been a reason. But she couldn't explain it. Words dried on her lips, thoughts vanished like ghosts in her mind.

The walls around her changed again. The gnarled wooden faces melted into hard stone faces: stone griffins, stone ants, stone snakes and goblins and dragons. She scrutinized them, wondering if one of the faces would move and be the source of the voice she heard in her head.

But none of the faces moved, nor did the voice speak again. There was utter silence. And when the silence had lasted for several minutes, Anya watched in disbelief as the glowing wasps' nest on Alum's lap began to dim, its light fading into darkness.

Once the light of the nest had gone, everything in the cavern was pitch black. Anya could neither see nor hear her companions. She could grope along through the passageway, but wondered if that would make any difference. The thought struck her: *I will die here.*

The sword was out of its sheath before Anya realized what she was doing. The blade was sharp; Alaric had always taken good care of it. And Anya knew she could brace the sword against the walls of the cave before she needed use of it. It wouldn't be hard for the steel to cut through her soft flesh. She took off her breast plate and her greaves, but she didn't brace the sword. She felt resolved, but still she hesitated. Taking a deep breath and closing her eyes, she wanted this moment to last for eternity. Perhaps her breath would never exhale, perhaps she could always be in this very moment, in the darkness of this cave.

"You will not die here."

The voice was not in her head this time. It came from close by, from a little further up the tunnel. It was low and rumbling, a mountain-deep voice. And with it came the glimmering of two green eyes, large and almond-shaped. The voice and the eyes had a body and limbs; the body walked upright and was as tall as a man, though Anya was beginning to see that it was not human. It held out one of those limbs, and resting in the palm of a velveted paw was an oval shape that glowed. The glow grew stronger, and the creature came closer, and when it was very close Anya could see clearly that it was some kind of feline, though its face reminded her more of a bull than of a lion. It wore a long robe, patterned with images of eyes and mouths and tongues. And the glowing oval in its paw was not a gem or a crystal. It was a dragon's eye.

And then the eye looked at her.

Anya trembled. The creature advanced towards her, holding the eye out in front like an offering. As it drew closer,

Anya could see just how large the cat-like monster was; if it resembled a man, it resembled one of prodigious height. It towered over her now, almost seven feet tall, and it held the glowing dragon's eye level with Anya's face. She could see nothing but the dragon's eye and the illuminated face of the cat peering down at her and frowning.

"Why have you come?" said the cat with its thick, bull-like lips, the voice deep and purring.

"I-- I don't know..."

"You do."

"Lord Brecken's men— To escape!"

The lips of the cat curled into a vicious snarl. Its teeth were bared, but only for a moment, then it purred again. It was a louder purr this time and not particularly friendly. It reminded Anya of a swarm of bees about to strike.

"I came because..."

"Not because. You came. And you brought these men with you. And now they are part of this place, just as you are part of this place. And we are all together part of this place."

The light from the dragon eye flashed brighter than two thousand torches, blinding Anya with its flare. But when her eyes adjusted and the white spots were blinked away, she could see the entire cavern now, with Alum, Tark, and Gilfore still where she'd left them, all three sitting on the cold dirt floor, unmoving, silent, eyes open and utterly blank. They looked like dead men who had not yet bothered to lay down and die. They were no more alive than a lump of stone or a log, thought their breath still came in and out of their lungs. But they were moss on a tree, slugs under a rock, barnacles on the hull of a long-sunken ship.

"Why didn't that happen to me?" Anya asked the cat. "Why was there no enchantment upon my mind?"

The cat's eyes widened. Its lips curled into a grin. "Why would the enchanter lay a spell upon herself?"

At first the creature's words meant nothing. It wasn't the answer she had expected, and so for a brief moment the meaning of what was said had passed over her mind. But the words lingered, and when they dropped at last into Anya's consciousness, she understood them, and she hated them in her disbelief.

"But I'm not!" A new theory filled her head. "You are the enchantment! This is *my* curse!"

"Do you feel giddy?" said the cat.

Anya had to admit that her revelation gave her some measure of satisfaction, that she was almost glad to know she would soon suffer the same fate as her companions. Being left out had been more disturbing, in its own way, than being cursed.

"The giddiness will flee," the cat continued. "It always does. And then the gloom comes."

But Anya didn't feel giddy. And the satisfaction of knowing that she too would fall under some terrible spell soured into disappointment. She knew she was not enchanted. She knew that what had happened to Gilfore and the others was *not* happening to her. It would never happen to her.

"What are you?" the cat said.

Anya didn't answer. She swallowed the truth that was beginning to bubble within her throat.

"Why did you come?"

Anya looked at her empty hands. There had never been a bag of gold. No soldiers. Had Alaric even been real? But he was her brother. She was wearing his armor, had stolen his sword, had watched him lay in the grass and stare at nothing. He had looked so sad before she stole everything from him. Then he had looked like nothing.

Anya looked desperately at the men around her. They were still there. They were not nothing. But the whites of their eyes seemed to grow wider, and their faces were pale and wan in the light of the dragon's eye. They were so still they might as well have been nothing.

"I did not come," she said at last.

The cat nodded.

"I have always been here."

"Yes." The cat smiled. "What are you?"

"I don't know."

"That is true. You do not know. Yet." The creature's eyes flashed. The cavern was illuminated with sparks of emerald green, and for a moment, Anya thought she saw the dragon's eye lift up into the air, a floating bubble in the eery light. But the eye wasn't floating; it was fixed now within the eye socket of a green-scaled dragon. The dragon's long neck swiveled back and forth like the body of a snake, then all of its green scales and its glowing eyes melted like one over-burned wax candle.

And there was darkness, but only for a moment. In the end of that moment, the teeth that had belonged to the cat smiled, and the green eyes gleamed. But these features were framed in a face that was not the cat's. It was a small figure, dwarfish in size, and thin and reedy as a broom-hag in autumn. It could have been a man, but Anya wasn't sure. Something about its size and its lumpy, pock-marked skin made her think of a toad.

"What are you?" This time Anya asked the question.

Same as you. The voice she heard was in her head and outside her head too. It was a man's voice, weathered by age and time and long years of sadness.

"I am nothing," Anya replied.

Exactly, the voice echoed in her head. *But you were not always so. You once were ordinary. But somehow, in some way, and because of some whim of your spirit, you were overcome by melancholia. By an unearthly, unwieldy grimness that you could not explain. Would not explain. For to explain it meant a kind of death, and you were not willing to die.*

Anya could say nothing, but she knew that what the voice spoke was true. The three men seated around her were men no more; only their bones waited in the darkness, tableau skeletons in repose. The boney jaws chattered as a heavy wind whispered through cavern. The little, reedy toad-like man who had stood before her and spoke inside her head was gone. He was the cat again, then he was a dragon's eye, then he too was gone. And Anya was gone. The darkness was gone. The cave walls were stone, then they were flesh, then they were dripping wet. It had been a century since she had walked through mouth of the cavern of Drys-Gul. Even the sword and the armor were gone, ground into dust—not by time—but by the gloom.

———

Drys-Gul was a gloom wizard.

What *is* a gloom wizard? This is the wrong question. To define a gloom wizard is only incidental. What a gloom wizard does is of much more consequence.

A gloom wizard does not practice some obscure form of sorcery; she (or he) is often an ordinary wizard to start. But the gloom wizard is not typical in all things. No, she (or he) is overcome with an unearthly, unwieldy spirit of melancholy. The anguish, despair, and unrelenting sadness of the person is such that a mystic sort of gloominess descends upon them, imbuing them with a supernatural, almost god-like state of melancholia, and it is this power which transforms the ordinary wizard into the gloom wizard.

After a time, this anguished state results in the dissolving of the human form into some other physical manifestation: a gnarled tree, a decrepit castle, a sulfur-breathing cave.

Or a thief in stolen armor.

A HEART MADE FOR BARGAINING

J ack Lightning felt the mists of morning against his pale skin. He was sneaking through the swamp in what should have been a messy business, but Jack loved the muck. Not too long ago, he had inherited a pair of tall leather boots, tough as seal-skin, black as tar, so it was a pleasure to let them slosh in the inky mire. And the swamp was the shortest way. Jack always loved a short cut.

"Quiet, Twitch," he said to the black and white stray inside his knapsack. The poor mangy cat was meowing nervously. Its green-yellow eyes didn't like the water curdling below. Water was the enemy. Jack scratched the cat's head just behind the ears, but Twitch didn't like it and pulled away, sinking back down into the darkness of the knapsack.

"We're almost there," said Jack. He slid his finger and thumb along the wide brim of his suede hat. The battered old thing had been with him from the time he was just a skinny urchin on the docks of Amberstone. He knew it was starting to come apart at the seems, and he knew it stunk of sweat and grease, but he couldn't part with it. It was as much a part of himself as his skin or his teeth. Besides, it kept him warm in the cold, wet mush of this swamp. And it kept his eyes shaded. Better for tricking. Never let your enemies or your marks see your eyes. And he had the biggest mark of his life on the other side of this swamp.

The Old Heron was waiting. It was still hard for Jack to believe that the time had finally come. He allowed his left hand to wade softly into his trouser pocket, feeling the orb inside. *What a price I paid to get this one, eh?* he thought. The orb was smooth but irregular in shape—it was almost spherical, but somehow one half had decided to bulge a little more than the other, giving it the impression of a globe that had gone saggy. Jack didn't take it out of his pocket, but he knew that by this time it was already glowing. The Heron would be happy. The orb was getting ripe.

The murky water was getting deeper and deeper with every step. Soon it splashed up around Jack's waist, forcing him to adjust his knapsack so that it hung across his shoulders, away from the swirling blackness below. Twitch wouldn't appreciate getting wet, and Jack didn't fancy facing the Heron without his lucky cat. For the Old Heron—fierce, battle-scarred, and bitter—hated only one thing. The feline species. Cats made the Heron squawk. Twitch meowed and squirmed inside the knapsack. Jack wondered if the cat knew where they were headed.

"Not long now," Jack said. "Got a fine tree for you to climb." The Heron's tree was fine, that much was true. But Twitch wouldn't be doing much climbing. If Jack was lucky, they'd trade the orb and be gone before the Heron even opened both eyes.

If I'm lucky. Jack smiled. He was always lucky.

Eventually, Twitch stopped squirming and Jack knew he was asleep. *Better for him,* he thought. *Let him rest before the work begins.*

The swamp started to empty. Reeds and lilies started getting thicker. Jack sliced his way through the thicket with his knife. The ground rose steadily now; Jack's boots found spongy footing as they made their way up the banks of the swamp. Soon the thick black boots were traipsing over wet earth and brown leaves. Thin, young saplings—the ones nearest the swamp—gave way to massive, ancient trees. Jack had found his way to the Herne at last.

The trees in the Herne were older than the mountains. They were the first things of the world, twisted and tall, trunks as wide as a giant's ass. The trees gave off a smell of must, like a cabinet full of parchments and scrolls kept in the cellar of a witch. Jack sucked in the musty air. It was going to be a long journey to the nests of the herons.

———

It didn't take more than a few hundred steps through the Herne before Jack met with his first obstacle. He knew the forest was filled with robbers and thieves, but to meet the king of the robbers on his first jaunt was quite a feat. Old Nog with legs as long as tall oaks stepped out from behind a tree and doffed his cap. He grinned his grin of three teeth and Jack knew that there was no way to escape what fate was in store.

"Evenin', gent," said Old Nog, whose face was as gnarled as a rotten turnip. He spit as he spoke and the soil sizzled from the poison therein. "You can't pass this way until you pay the fee to Old Nog."

"I have nothing to give," was Jack's reply, but Nog could see that was a lie. Jack wanted to put his hand in his pocket and feel the smoothness of the orb, but he didn't dare. He kept his cool.

But Nog asked for something else.

"Give me that fine coin purse that hangs from your shoulder."

Jack prayed to all the gods he could name in his silent head that Twitch would keep still. The cat, thankfully, did not stir. *Sleeping, I'd wager.*

"Aye, that coin purse, as you say, is fine indeed," Jack replied. "But it's filled with nothing but scraps of food, and what care you for poor man's food when all this forest feeds your hunger. You, sir, need something worth something. You need treasure."

"I'll take that coin purse, whippersnapper, if you don't mind," said Old Nog, and he stretched out his boney fingers like the legs of a spider, straining to stick their tips onto Jack's bag.

"Ah, but!" cried Jack, taking a step back.

"But what?" said Nog, his rheumatic eyes narrowing.

"But what about my boots?" Jack lifted his left foot to show off the slick black leather. Even covered in the muck of the swamp, the boots looked fine as a bottle of ink.

Old Nog stared at the boots and ideas took root in his mind. He had such long legs—they would be needing a good pair of boots someday. Why not today? Nog's own feet were bare as the rocks, colored brown by leaf and lichen. What he would look like in those fine leather things. What a stride he would make.

"Give me those boots," said Old Nog, "and I'll let you pass. I might even let you live, if they fit me right and don't cause a callous."

Though he hated to part with the boots, Jack knew this was a good deal. He pulled them from his feet and gave them to the old man. Now Jack's feet were bare as anything, and Nog walked around with the slick, fine boots on his legs—the boots looking like leeches that had crawled up the trunks of two wobbly trees.

Jack trudged off, feeling with a wince every twig and pebble. But Old Nog was satisfied and didn't even see Jack go. Twitch never made a movement nor even a purr.

"Better to lose the boots than you, my friend," Jack said to the cat in the bag over his shoulder, but the cat never heard.

Jack spent the next hundred steps fingering the orb in his pocket, making sure it was still there. Before long, he heard the soft gurgle of a stream. Running along through the trees was a creek, muddy and shallow. Sitting on the edge of it was a raggedy woman, her hair stringy as ivy vines, her clothes the same color as the brown water. Her back was to Jack. She sat dangling her barefoot feet above the flowing water, humming softly a dark tune. Jack had a good ear for music, and he could hear a minor key as quick as a bird. He tried to step away from the creek and the woman, but twigs snapped and ground betrayed him. She whirled her head in an instant, and cut off her last note like an axe falling on a prisoner's neck.

Jack almost wretched at the sight of her face. Pock-marked and shriveled, her face had little maggots crawling in and out of the open sores and punctures which littered her cheeks. Her eyes were wider than a cat's because the skin around them had thinned and stretched back to her temples. She grinned and her teeth were knife-sharp. Her voice carried the same dark tone as her song.

"Well met and fine greetings, my fair man," she said. "Come to hear me sing? I love to have an audience. Come, sit by me and dip your feet into the waters if you can. I won't bite."

Something about those teeth made Jack doubt it. "Afraid I can't stop now," he said, doffing his hat in a gentlemanly way. "Perhaps on my return, we'll share a duet."

The hag laughed. "You lie as good as a jackal! But somehow, I have a hunch that you won't pass by this way again. Come then and sit by me. I won't bite, I swear it on the moon!"

"The moon, madam? The moon is ever-changing. I can't trust an oath by the moon."

"But I am of the moon and the moon is of me. How can a lady not swear by the very stuff of herself? For I am Maggie o' the Moon, fairest lady of that fair orb."

Jack stiffened at the word. *Did she know? But no, of course she could not know.* Jack's hand relaxed.

"Forgive me, madam, I did not know."

"That's alright my handsome jack, for if you sit with me and sing a while, I'll be satisfied."

Jack needed to think fast. He saw a trap as true as ever, but how to throw her off the scent.

"May I leave a marker in my stead?" he asked at last. "A token of my good word and a pledge to come back this way again when time is more to my liking?"

Maggie o' the Moon let her smile drop. Somehow, despite the closing of her mouth and the disappearance of her hideous teeth, she looked more frightening. Her sadness was worse than her fake mirth.

"I suppose it had better be something worth having, if I can't have my fancy man here beside me," she pouted.

"Madam, take a few coins from my purse," Jack offered.

Maggie o' the Moon scoffed. "Am I worth nothin' to you but a few farthings?" Then her face turned dark and scowled. This was the worst face of all. It was like watching the moon eclipse and the face of it turn blood red. She began to get up from her spot by the riverbank. She looked ready to bite.

"Alright, alright!" Jack tried to stem her anger. "You name the thing! I'll give you whatever you ask!"

This mollified her for a moment. She sat back down with a soft thud and grew pensive. She leered at Jack then, looking him up and down. "Ah me," she muttered, "so much worth taking." She licked her lips.

Jack suppressed as much of a shudder as he could. He wondered what magic this hag might have and if she could see into his pockets. Just then Twitch meowed and fidgeted around in the bag.

"What's this, what's this!" Maggie shrieked. "A kitty for Maggie to play with?"

Twitch kept struggling, so Jack had no choice but to open

his bag and lift the wriggling feline out. Poor Twitch was jumpy and didn't expect to see another face, particularly not one so hideous as Maggie's. It took all of Jack's effort to not let the poor cat slip from his fingers. Then complete terror took him as he realized Maggie might ask for the cat. *She'd just as soon eat him as give him a pat,* he thought.

But Maggie's face soured when she saw the scrawny black-and-white. "Nay, a mangy thing is that!" she spat. "Barely worth picking my teeth afterward." She grinned and ground her razor-like teeth together.

Jack smoothed Twitch's fur and hummed a little ditty to the poor, nervous wreck until at last he calmed and purred. "Agreed," Jack said, "he's much too sickly. Not right in the head, in fact." He placed the cat back in the knapsack.

"But Maggie is still owed, she is."

"That's right."

The hag licked her lips again and squinted at Jack's belly. "And the hour is getting time for supper."

Jack took a slight step back. He kept his fingers lively, just in case he needed to reach for his knife. "Not too late, I think. There's still some time for merriment yet."

"Aye, for merriment..." She started to get up, to creep toward Jack. The worms crawling in and out of her face were slithering faster now. Jack could see her claws more clearly too. Each finger had a long nail that look like the edge of jagged knife.

Jack gulped. *If only I didn't have to look at that hideous face,* he thought. *But I can barely stand to glance in that direction without feeling sick. Poor Maggie needs a proper bag on her head.* Then he had a sudden thought.

"My lady!" he bowed graciously. "I have suddenly thought on the perfect gift for your fair form!" He took off his hat and doffed it, then held it out for Maggie to see. Jack's hat was one of his oldest possessions, a fine deep blue leather with a peacock quill in the sash. Its brim was wide and it conformed with supple grace to his head. That hat had been with him through thick and thin. But it was still beautiful, despite the wear and weathering of its many years. *And Maggie's face, perhaps, could be shielded a bit by the wide brim...*

"My hat, gentle madam of the moon," he continued, "is a gift as fine as any for so sweet a lady as yourself. I offer it to you now, in my stead. For though I cannot stay and sit with you, my hat at least will comfort your head." He held the hat to her.

Maggie looked at the hat curiously. Her head cocked, her eyes unsearchable, Jack didn't know what to make of it. *Does she like the offer?* She started creeping toward him again. Jack held the hat with one hand but began to move his other hand towards the knife hidden under his shirt. She clinked her long fingernails together. Jack had his hand on his knife. One quick move and he could have it out and in her gut the minute she came upon him. But as Maggie drew closer and closer, her fingers did not go for his throat. They reached out to caress the soft leather hat. She drew one hand over the long, fuzzy peacock feather. She gingerly lifted the hat from Jack's hands and placed it on her head.

"Ah!" she said as the hat melted into her head and slouched a bit to one side, obscuring part of her face. "So soft! I bet as soft as yer belly," she added with an ugly wink.

"It suits you well. Better than it ever suited me."

"Mmmm," Maggie said as she preened and paraded in her new hat. "Tis true, tis true! I like it well. I'll take this for my bargain and let you leave in peace." She ran her fingers along the brim and smiled like a child who had gotten away with some mischief. "But if ever you pass this way again..." She flashed her teeth once more with lusty hunger. "... I shall insist you sit beside me on the bank." Then with a hiss and a girlish squeak, she capered back over to her perch above the creek and sat down to dangle her feet once more.

Boots gone, hat gone, Jack felt quite naked now. *Still,* he thought, *my cat's in my knapsack and my treasure's still in my pocket. I don't need boots or a hat to meet with the Old Heron.*

The forest grew quite thick and darker the further he traveled. The little clearing and the flowing creek seemed a world away now. Even hideous Maggie seemed less terrifying than the shadows and darkness that closed in upon him as he headed into the very center of the Herne.

Twitch meowed.

"Yes, I hear it too, friend," said Jack. There was a whistling of wind through the thick trees. It had a high sound, like the weeping of banshees. Jack knew something was watching them. He looked up into the tops of the trees. *Perhaps we've found the Heron,* he thought. But there were no nests up there. Just a canopy of thick leaves that blocked out any trace of sunlight. Jack looked about him, trying to peer into the gaps and spaces between the trees and underbrush. But there was nothing save black shadows. Not even an animal stirred in this part of the forest. And yet, something followed them. Something stalked.

Twitch was restless now. He wriggled in the knapsack and Jack feared he might scratch the leather to ribbons. So Jack began to sing. It was a whispered song at first, just a mumbled string of melodies. But then one of the melodies caught his mind and he began to find the words.

"Away, away, cried the maiden dear," Jack sang as softly as he dared. "For in this land is naught but tears. I canna leave, the sailor said, for I do love thee in my stead. Too'la, too'la, too'la, la'rey, the sailor kissed her on the quay. He kissed her on the quay."

Twitch was satisfied. He purred and settled down. Jack stopped his song after a few more quiet verses.

"Dooooonnnn't sssssstoooopppppp....." something hissed into the silence.

Jack froze. He looked around to see what had spoken, but all was blackness and unmoving trees.

"Doooooonn't ssssssstoooopppppp....." the scratching voice said again. "Sssssiiiiinnng agaaaaaain...."

"I—" Jack started. The voice was bone-chilling, creeping down his spine like a long knife. He could hardly breathe let along form words or song. *What is it? Where is it? This cannot be the Old Heron. This is something else.*

"Sssssiiiiinnng!" the hissing voice demanded.

Jack couldn't think of a single note.

"Yoooour faaaaccce is faaaair, yoooour eyessssss are bluuuue," the chilling hiss said. It seemed so much closer now, like it was breathing down Jack's neck. "Sssssiiiiing that ssssoooonnnng or the Gruesome will devoooour you."

Jack summoned every ounce of courage he could muster. This took more courage than his fight against the dreaded sea captain of the Red Wenches. This took more courage than the harsh years he spent living and stealing on the streets. This took more courage and cunning than the whole year spent finding and fighting to keep the orb in his pocket. Something about that formless voice was fear personified. It was fear speaking to him from the heart of the Herne, the fear that probably birthed the trees themselves. The hidden fear of this ancient place. The Gruesome, it had called itself. Jack had never heard of such a creature, but now, having heard its horrible voice, he would never forget it.

"Away, away—" Jack began, but his voice caught in his throat. He cleared it and hoped the Gruesome would not mind. "Away, cried the maiden lost. For in the sea you must be tossed. I will'na leave, the sailor said, for I do love thee in my stead. Too'la, too'la, too'la, too'low, the sailor kissed her and would not go. Away, away, the maiden mewed. For the ancient fighting's been renewed. I shall not leave, the sailor called, for I do love thee best of all. Too'la, too'la, too'la, too'rey, the sailor died that very day."

"Yeeesssss," hissed the voice. "You havvvve caaaauuught the meeaaassssuuuure of it. Sssssiiiiiiinnng agaaaaainnn."

Jack couldn't believe the words he spoke in reply. "But that is the end of the song. The sailor is dead. There's no more to sing."

The voice hissed with rage, a long, high-pitched sound. "Nnnoooooooo!" it cried. "Ssssssiiiiiiinnng agaaaaaainnnn!"

I have sealed my death! Jack thought in a panic. His entire body began to tingle now, as if centipedes and spiders crawled all over him, as if little pricks of needles were dancing on his skin. He writhed and shuddered. The Gruesome was closer, he could feel it closing in.

"I cannot!" Jack cried. "My fear prevents me!"

The voice laughed. It was like the crackling of fire. "Fffffeeeeeaaarrrr.... Yeeeeessssss... Now, I shaaaallll ssssiiiinnnng... The Gruesome shaaaaallll haaavvvve hisssssss supper..."

It was impossible to tell where the creature was coming from. There was still nothing to see in that dark forest. But Jack could feel an even darker shadow overtaking him, he could sense the hot breath and the wet mouth of something huge opening its maw to devour him. He tried to sing. He tried desperately. But the words would not come. The tune was lost. And so was he.

The Gruesome—hidden, invisible, larger than the largest snake and yet unseen—was about to close its formless jaws around the man and his cat and the secret treasure stowed away in his pocket. And then Jack tried a gambit that only desperate men can make. He bargained.

"What about a gift instead of a song?" he bellowed into the unseen mouth that was going to eat him.

Suddenly, the air was a bit fresher. The hot steam of the Gruesome's throat was momentarily gone.

"A giiiiiffffft?" it said.

"Aye, a gift. You'll like this one." Jack reached under his shirt and took out the knife hidden there. "This knife, you see, is no ordinary knife." That much was true, in fact. The knife was the first thing Jack had ever stolen, back when he was just an urchin living on the streets of Farrow Town. His mother dead by the plague, his father killed by the king's men, Jack was only ten and alone. He stole the knife because he knew he needed steel in order to live in the bleak and dangerous world. He stole it from a fat inn keeper who let him sleep in the pig sty. He stole it and stabbed the inn keeper. His first murder.

But the knife had served him well. It proved a fine instrument to keep a boy safe, and later to aid a man in his thievery. The Gruesome would have no love for such a gift, Jack knew. But all this story is not what Jack told to the creature.

"Whyyyyy woooould I waaaaannnnt a kniiiiffffe?" the Gruesome hissed.

"You loved the song, eh? Well this knife is the token of that sad and lovely tale. For the poor sailor had bled from the blade of this very knife. The song I sang was true, you see. And this knife is the proof of it. Look here," Jack said, pointing at a little speck on the blade. "The sailor's blood, sure as I am standing here. And if you listen closely, you can hear the blood still singing. In fact, it was from the blood on this knife that I first heard the song you so love. And if I give the knife to you now, it will sing for you, and perhaps one day you may sing the song yourself. What greater gift could I give you? For I am a man, and my voice will one day give out, and you'll never hear the tune again from me. But if you take this knife and let it sing for you, then you'll have the song forever."

There was no sound. No movement. Jack almost wondered if the Gruesome had gone away. But then he heard air seep out from nowhere, like the trees exhaling. The Gruesome sighed.

"Yyyeeeessssss..." it said at last. "I will taaaaake it."

"Ah, but how can I give it to you if you remain unseen?"

The Gruesome hissed again, an angry hiss like a kettle boiling over. But then, upon the moist, dark earth, the thing appeared. It was like a snake, and like a swan with its long curved neck, and like a bat too in its eyes and pointed ears. It was longer than the trunks of the trees. Its entire body encircled Jack and its long neck towered and swayed above him, the face and rodent-like eyes peering dangerously close to Jack's own.

"Heeeeaaarrrr it ssssiiiiinnng," said the Gruesome. Both the top and bottom of its mouth had two sharp rows of teeth.

Jack had found his courage and his voice again. He held up the knife, and with his lips barely moving, began to sing softly. "Away, away, cried the maiden dear, for in this land is naught but tears..." It was a satisfying ruse, for it seemed the knife was singing.

"Yyyeeeeessssss!" smiled the Gruesome.

"But, my friend, how shall you keep this knife?" Jack said, warming up to his part. "For you have no hands nor a belt to hold it? I tell you what you shall do. Open that wide mouth of yours again, and I shall put the knife there. Perhaps if you keep the knife in your mouth, it will sing the words of the song for you there. Now open wide that I may place it in."

The Gruesome nodded. Jack heaved back and with all his strength and aim, hurled the knife into the mouth and down the throat of the huge creature. The Gruesome snapped its jaw shut, and as it did, the knife streaked down its gullet. Jack could see the sharp object outlined in the Gruesome's swan-like neck. The creature tried to swallow it down farther, to get it into its belly. But the more the Gruesome struggled, the tighter its neck became. The knife's blade poked through the thin neck. The Gruesome tried to cough it up, but that only pulled things tighter. With one final choke, the Gruesome pushed the knife blade right through its neck, the silver steel piercing through the flesh, black hot blood squirting out the puncture. The Gruesome flung its neck back and forth, its head lolling to either side. It tried to screech, but that just pushed the knife out further. The sound of its hissing was caught there, cut upon the knife.

Jack wasted no time. He ran. He clutched the knapsack and secured the orb and never looked back to see if the Gruesome had stopped breathing.

When he stopped running, he collapsed upon the ground. He lay there for a while with eyes closed, listening for any sound that the Gruesome had followed. He listened for danger. All was silent. Then he opened his eyes and saw, high up in the highest tree, a huge nest and a thick pale yellow beak peering over it.

The Old Heron.

———

THERE WERE NO OTHER NESTS IN THE TREES. UNLIKE other herons Jack had seen, the Old Heron did not live in a heronry. He lived alone. It didn't take long for the Old Heron to emerge. His long, s-shaped neck rose from the shaggy nest, displaying the plumes of wispy feathers on his chest. His body was more grey now than blue, but his head still had a bold streak of black above his eyes and long feathers that sprouted from his head and hung down his back like stray hairs. His eyes made Jack catch his breath. They were as yellow as dandelions with just a pin-prick of black in the center of each. They caught Jack in their glare and never released him.

The heron descended from his nest like a hot air balloon deflated to the ground, his huge wings spread out to catch the air currents as he fell. He floated down to a long-hanging branch of the tree and perched there. His height, his long legs, his fine snake-like neck were on full display. He was the largest bird Jack had ever seen, and he had spent time with vultures and eagles. But the heron was greater than even those, his long years upon the earth making him a massive, ancient giant. All he did was stare at Jack with those unblinking, unnatural yellow eyes. Now that the Heron was closer, Jack could see just how thick and sharp the bird's beak was. It was like a dagger's blade.

Anyone who got on the end of that beak would find a hole in his gullet, Jack thought. *And here I am without a knife.*

Jack waited for the bird to make a sound, to squawk or croak at him, but the Heron was silent. He just sat there on the low-hanging branch and stared directly at Jack. Then a sort of grumble started in the back of the Heron's throat. It sounded like the start of his squawk, but nothing came out of his beak. Jack had a moment of panic; the look of the bird, the strange noise — they could all be leading up to one quick stab of his beak and that would be the end of Jack Lightning. He needed to act fast. He took out the orb.

As soon as Jack held up the glowing, oblong sphere, the Heron screeched a hideous croaking cry.

"Aaaarwk! Aaaarwk! Aaaawrk!" The Old Heron beat his huge wings and the force of them felt like a high wind against Jack's face. Jack thought for sure that the Heron was about to dive at him, stab him with that thick, sharp beak, and start eating his entrails. But Jack held firm and clutched the orb with steady fingers. The Old Heron settled down, but his long neck extended as close as it could toward the orb. The Heron's eyes — so unmoving, so blank before — were now glinting with hunger.

"So," the bird began. His voice was not human; it scraped like sandpaper scratched over iron. "You found it at last."

Jack found his voice. "Aye. I'm ready to make the deal."

"Why should this bird make a deal? Why not just take the sweet egg from you? Cut you open with this bird's beak." The Heron clicked his beak together like a pair of scissors.

"You wouldn't want to try," Jack said. He reached over his shoulder and unslung the knapsack. "I've got my own weapon." He opened the sack and pulled out Twitch. When the little cat saw the Heron, he gave a hiss, and the Heron jerked his neck back. He flapped his wings and let out another cry of angry "arwks."

Jack put the cat away. "Well done," he whispered to Twitch as he closed the bag again. "Now stay alert. We're not done yet."

The Heron had settled down. "This bird sees you are clever. That is so. This bird will not cut you open." He gained his confidence back and leaned back in toward the orb. "The egg means no use to you. The egg is food for this bird. This bird can make a deal then."

"I'm glad," said Jack.

"What is your offer? This bird will hear it."

Jack had been rolling the words over in his mind ever since he first heard the legend of the Old Heron. Give it a rare gift, give it the food it desires, and the Old Heron will answer you questions three: your fate, your time, your heart's desire.

"I want your answers to the questions three," he said to the bird.

The Heron squawked again, turning his head upward and bellowing his shouts to the treetops. Then he shook his head and the white plume on his neck and chest shook like tall grass in the wind.

Jack waited for the Heron to speak, but the bird was silent now and staring again with his bright yellow eyes. "What is my fate?" Jack said at last. "How shall I die?"

The Heron said nothing.

"What is my time? When shall I die?" Jack waited, but the Heron made no response.

"Will I find my heart's desire? Shall I ever have a lady love?"

The Heron said nothing, and Jack had a wicked feeling that the stories weren't true. This bird wasn't anything special, just a strange creature that lived alone in an old forest. But then the Heron croaked and it was a terrible broken sound. It rolled its yellow eyes back into its head.

"You shall die by the cut of a blade," the Heron began. "When the truth is swallowed, then your neck will bleed. And yes, you'll find your lady love. When the sun comes by another name."

Then the Heron's eyes rolled back to face Jack and the

bird glared at him. "This bird wants his meal," the Heron hissed. "Give it!"

Jack held the orb up as far as he could. He'd lost about an inch when he gave up his boots, but the long neck of the Heron was able to dip down far enough to reach the orb. With its thick, strong beak, the Heron pecked at the orb like a hammer coming down steel. Each time the beak pounded on the orb, Jack felt his hand and his arm rattle. He was just about to stop the Heron and set the orb down when the thing cracked. The Heron pulled back, its eyes both hungrily staring and gaping in awe.

"Yes!" the bird cried.

Jack stared in disbelief as well. The orb cracked open and crawling out from it was a tiny starfish that glowed with phosphorescent light. Jack caught his breath at the beauty of it. The little starfish pulsed and waved its tentacles while it mewed a strange, innocent hum.

The Heron clacked its beak together twice and lunged at the glowing starfish. In one quick snap, the beak had closed around the delicate little body, and the light was snuffed out. The Heron swallowed the starfish whole.

Jack felt sick. He had traded that poor creature's life for a few riddling words. Twitch meowed in the knapsack. The Heron cawed and flapped angrily when it heard the cat.

"Twitch," said Jack, thinking of what would happen now if he took the cat out and let the feline have his way with the bird. His hands were close to pulling the sack open. But then he stopped himself. No use. What's done is done.

The Heron seemed to laugh at Jack's sickened face.

"What did you think you were bringing this bird?" the Heron said. "Your human heart is weak to mourn over meat."

Jack had no answer. The Old Heron croaked again and then flew back up to his nest high in the tree.

Jack took the broken pieces of the orb's shell and let them fall to the ground. Twitch was silent.

————

JACK LIGHTNING FELT THE SMOKEY BREATH OF THE FIRE burn his eyes.

"You're sitting too close, lad," said a grizzled old drinker a few tables away. "Pull up next to us here, get yourself out of the smoke."

But Jack didn't feel like making old men happy or making himself more comfortable. He wanted to feel the sting of the smoke.

Twitch was on his lap, snoring softly and curled up into a little black and white ball of fur. Jack took one last gulp of his ale and then waved the serving wench to his side.

"More," he coughed.

The poor girl tried to smile and be friendly, but Jack could tell she was disgusted by his miserable state. He was drunk, no doubt about that. He hadn't moved from that spot for fourteen hours. He looked wilder than an ape and a bit crazy too. No shoes, no hat to cover his rain-soaked, greasy hair. The haggard look of a man who had been traveling through all manner of storm and wilderness. *I think she only comes near because of the cat*, he thought as he watched the serving girl go to the barkeep and fill up Jack's tankard.

When she returned, she tried smiling again. "A bowl of broth next?" she said gently. "How about a bed?"

Jack took the tankard of ale and resumed his essential task of staring listlessly into the fire. The girl left without another word.

It was so alive, he thought. *Like a star come down from the heavens. Such beauty! It had to have been magic. No other explanation. There's no natural creature on this earth that could look the way that starfish looked. None. And I sent it to the bottom of the belly of that monstrous bird. For what? For a bunch of meaningless garble. A stupid, selfish string of words that mean nothing. No, even worse. I gave up that thing of beauty for LESS than nothing.*

"You shall die by the cut of a blade," the Heron had said.

Jack laughed to himself. *Of course I'll die by the blade. I've lived by nothing else.* Slowly the memories crept into the corners of his waking mind. He blocked them out as well as he could, but they kept seeping in like the smoke from the fire. The flash of his knife. The scream of the poor man. The glow. The pulsing beat as he held it in his hand.

"It was just luck," he said out loud. *Just luck. Yes.* He took another swallow of his ale and let the memories drain down his throat.

"Excuse me, sir." The serving girl was back. Jack's eyes could hardly focus now, but through the haze he could make out a sweet face. Soft eyes. Hair the color of honey. "Sir," she said again. "Master Ben says we need to get you to bed." She seemed to indicate the barkeep. He was behind his counter, wiping it down and looking annoyed at Jack's presence. "You're falling asleep anyway, sir. You'll spill your drink."

She tried to take the tankard from Jack and he didn't put up a fight. Her hair smelled of sage and a bit of rosemary. As her hands passed over his, he felt their softness. *Such softness for a tavern wench. Or am I dreaming again? Is this part of the memory?*

"Thank you," he managed to whisper.

"'Tis my pleasure," she replied. "Come on, puss." She picked up Twitch with a gentle touch and held the cat under one arm while she raised Jack up from his seat with the other.

"'Bout time!" the grizzled man at the nearby table sneered. "Throw him out with the pigs!"

"He stinks!" called another harsh voice.

"Crazed like the pixies in the Sundown Bog," cackled a woman's voice.

"Been to see the Devil, he has!" another drunk chimed in. "Throw him to the pigs!"

The serving girl said nothing. She helped Jack to a staircase. "Up this way," she said. She was stronger than Jack would have thought. She practically carried him up the stairs.

Soon he was floating on a bed made of down, the soft cotton sheets swaddling him like a babe in arms. Twitch was nuzzled into his neck, warm and purring.

"They call me Dawn," said the girl. "I'll be in to check on you. Get some rest."

Jack slept and dreamed of the starfish. He heard the voice of Dawn floating through all of his visions. Dawn. Like the morning sunrise. Like the promise of the new day. Like being born a second time. Dawn. Her voice and her honeyed hair mixed with the clean smell of his pillow. He watched as the glowing starfish faded and turned into her smiling face. He felt tears drip down his face. He snuggled into Twitch.

When he woke up, the room was cold. The fire had gone out. The only light came from the faint gray light of the moon shining through a lone window.

"Twitch," Jack croaked into the darkness. *My voice sounds like the Old Heron,* he thought. "Twitch!"

He felt the bed sheets for the cat, but they were empty. "Twitch!" He sat up.

"Don't move again," said a man's voice. It was low and soft, but the note of a threat hung from it like an icicle hanging from an eave. "Be still or you won't like what happens next."

"Where's Twitch?" Jack said, his voice low as well. He knew when things called for secrecy.

"Why ask that?" said the man. "You know we have him."

Jack did know, but he hoped it wasn't true. "He's just an old stray."

"He's more."

"I'll kill you." Jack tried desperately to think if there was anything in the room he could use as a weapon.

"With what? We know you have no blade. And we know you have no musket. We know you have nothing but a headache and a guilty heart."

Just then, Jack heard footsteps coming up the stairs. They made their way to the door of his room. He wanted to call out a warning. *Dawn!* he thought. *She's coming!*

"The serving wench!" hissed the hidden voice of the man. "Ready boys!"

Dawn opened the door, a taper in her hand, and Jack saw

as two shadowy men attacked her. They were quick. One had his hand over her mouth before she could scream. The other had a knife pointed toward her gut before she could move. The taper fell from her hand and the light was snuffed out.

"Quiet, lassie," said the grim voice in the dark. "Don't curse your luck."

"She's no part of this," Jack said. "Let her go."

"She'll yell for a constable. No, my lad. She's a part of things now."

Jack knew his words were hollow. "What is the cat to you? I need to know the truth before I hand him over."

The hoarse voice chuckled. "You want truth, eh? Tell me, Jack Lightning, how did you come by the orb of Etherel?"

Jack thought these robbers many things, but never in his wildest thoughts did he consider that they had a connection to the orb. He was speechless.

"That's what I thought, Bogg," said the man with his knife to the girl's gut. "He's as cowardly as they come."

"He's dangerous, Willy," said the man Bogg, the one who sat in the shadows. "But yes, a coward just the same."

Jack didn't have the strength nor the truth to defend his honor. He had only lies. "I won the orb by luck. What is it to you that I did? The man I won it from is dead."

"Aye, that he is, Jack Lightning. That he is."

Jack heard the croaking words of the Heron ring in his ears. You shall die by the cut of a blade. But why should the girl—Dawn—why should she suffer for him? And poor Twitch. Jack wondered if the cat was dead already.

"If you have Twitch, why are you still here? Why not just go and do with him what you will?"

"You would let us leave here alive with your precious feline? Somehow I think not. Somehow I think you'd come for us. Just as we have come here for you."

"The kitty's an extra bit of luck," said Willy. "You'se the one we come for."

"Silence!" hissed Bogg. "We haven't come here for Jack Lightning. We've come here for the truth. For a confession."

"I tell mine only to a priest," said Jack.

"You shall tell it to me," said Bogg. "Or your lassie here will bleed."

Jack could hear the girl struggle, but Willy and his comrade held her fast. She wasn't going to escape.

"If I tell you how I came by the orb, then you'll let her go? And what of the cat?"

"He stays with us. You know why, of course."

He's lucky, thought Jack. "I'll tell you half the truth," Jack bargained. "Then you let the girl go. Once she's safe, I'll tell you the other half."

No one spoke. No one moved. Jack knew that Bogg was considering the deal.

"She'll squeal!" whined Willy at last, breaking the uncomfortable silence.

"Nay, she'll be a good little girl, won't she," said the other man who had his sweaty hand over her mouth. He sniffed her and brushed his lips against her cheek. Jack was disgusted, but swallowed his anger.

"Begin," said Bogg.

Jack took a deep breath. He had never spoken these words out loud before. Even in his own head, he had drowned them with songs and drink and thoughts of treasure.

"I met the man on a boat, sailing for Eventon," he began. "He was sickly and the captain was sure he wouldn't last the journey. I tried to comfort him. He gave me his boots. Slick and black, they were. He said they were a gift... for giving him so much cheer and good companionship. I thought he would die. We all did. But then the ship reached harbor and we got off into the city, and the man didn't die. He coughed up blood and half his innards it seemed, but he didn't die, and none of us could explain it. I tried to give the boots back, when I saw that the man was going to recover. But he insisted and said to take them with his blessing."

"We didn't come for no tale about boots," sneered the greasy Willy.

"Shut it," snapped Bogg to Willy. The man kept quiet. "Keep on, Jacky boy," Bogg said to Jack.

"I kept the boots. I also took down the man's address. He said to see him any time for a good bit of ale and a song. He said he owned a shop, one of them alchemy shops, deep in the flea-bitten district of Eventon. I never thought I'd see him again."

"But you did," hissed Bogg.

"I did. I'm ashamed to say it. I needed money. I'm a thief and when a thief needs money, he goes to easy marks to get it. And the old man seemed one. Sickly, owned a shop. How could I know?" Jack's voice caught in his throat. He hated for the girl to hear him say such things. *Why should I care about her?* a bitter voice inside him cut in. *She means nothing to me. But no—the way she smiled, the honey-softness of her hair.*

Jack cared. Dawn was her name. Bright as the sun rising. And he hated for her to hear this tale.

"He's stalling!" Willy cried. "Watch him, Bogg! Let's just kill him and be over with it."

"No!" Bogg's voice was like an icicle shattering.

"Why do you want to hear all this anyway?" Jack dared. "I have half a feeling you know it all already."

Even in the darkness, Jack knew Bogg was smiling.

"I do," the man in the shadows said at last. "But I want to hear you say it. You're a dead man anyway, Jack Lightning. But to save the girl, you'll tell me the truth."

Jack spoke the words he'd never dared speak before. "I went into his shop. The Blood Moon, it was called. He welcomed me in, poured me a drink. We talked and sang sea shanties, and he asked me to stay the night. Said he had a spare room above the shop. I smiled and fingered my knife. I said I couldn't stay. I said I needed to be going. He saw the look in my eyes, and he knew. He pleaded a bit. Said that his wares were precious, not to take any. He offered me the coin in his coin box, said it was more than enough. But I'd gotten greedy. I'd eyed and been awed by all the treasures in his tiny shop. One in particular, one on a high shelf..."

"The orb," Bogg finished.

"Aye. The orb. It glowed and pulsed like it was alive and something about it made me remember a tale the sailors had told when I used to sail with the crew of the Grey Gull. They told a tale about the Old Heron, and the egg the Heron hungered for. 'Bring the Heron his glowing egg and he shall tell you your fortune.' I saw the orb there in the man's shop and somehow I knew. And the promises of the Old Heron echoed in my head. I was mad with desire for it. I lunged at the old man. He didn't even scream."

There was silence and Jack looked to the two men who held Dawn. "Let her go," he said. "The first half of the truth has been spoken."

"No," said Bogg. "The first half isn't done. Finish it. Say the words."

Jack looked at Dawn now. It was the first time he had looked at her since she'd come into the room. He could see her face, despite the darkness. It's the brightness in it, he thought. Her face glows like a candle. When he looked into her eyes, he saw them wide with fear. He knew then that she had no love for him. He had no fear to say the words.

"I killed the old man and took the orb without a word." He swallowed hard and the words went down like rocks in his throat.

"That is the first half of the truth," said Bogg. He must have signaled to his men, for in the next moment, Jack heard the sound of steel going into flesh, the muffled grunt of the girl as the robbers stabbed her in the belly. He could see her figure drop in a heap to the floor, a lifeless, heavy sack of bone and blood.

The "no" caught in his throat.

Bogg laughed. "She was dead the moment she stepped on that staircase."

"But I told you my half—"

"Yes, and now it is time for the other half."

"There is no more truth for me to speak," Jack said with venom. "I've told you everything."

"I'm sorry, Jack, but you're wrong," said Bogg. "You've only spoken half of the truth."

"I've told you everything!" Jack cried.

"Softly now, softly." Bogg laughed again, and then Jack heard the door creak open. He couldn't make out the face of the new figure, but something about the way the figure moved made Jack think it was someone with many years on his shoulders.

"You see, Jack," Bogg continued, "you've told us everything *you* know. That's true. But what you've told us is only half. The other half of the truth is standing here before you."

The figure who had just come into the room coughed. Jack knew that cough. It was wet, as if blood had been hacked up with it.

"Hello, Jack," said the voice of the figure. An old man. The alchemist shop. Jack had heard a voice from the grave.

"I killed you," Jack whispered.

"Yes, we heard you say that earlier," said the old man's voice. "And yet, how can you kill a man who knows how to cheat death? Who knows the hidden mysteries of science and alchemy? The real truth is that you stole from me. And now I'm here to get my goods back."

"But the orb..." Jack sputtered. "I already gave it to the Heron."

"Did you now?" said the old man between coughs. "No matter. It's a shame you don't have your knife anymore."

"Nor your hat," said Willy.

Jack's insides burned when he heard the voice of that murderer. He shot Willy a withering, hateful glance, though little good it did him in the dark. But even in the dark he could make out some details, and when he looked at Willy he thought he saw a hat on the man's head. A familiar hat, floppy and a bit dashing, worn by age but still soft suede...

No, Jack thought. *It can't be.*

"Nor your boots," said Bogg. "Though the boots were never yours to begin with, were they?" Bogg's clicked the heels of his own boots on the floor.

They aren't, they can't be, Jack thought. Then he remembered the knife in the third robber's hand, the one that had killed the poor girl.

Dawn was her name, Jack thought. *Her hair like honey.*

"Do you know, Jack?" said the old man, shuffling closer to Jack's position on the bed. "Do you know how I came by the orb in the first place?"

Jack had no more answers. He closed his eyes and tried to picture Dawn one last time. All he saw, instead, was the glowing starfish, soft and wavy like a feather in his hand.

"It wasn't very hard," the old man continued. "They can be found most readily for those willing to look for them. Since you stole mine, I find it is most appropriate for you to pay me back. You know my companions, I'm sure. There is Bogg, who happens to be wearing a fine pair of black leather boots. And Willy, here, is sporting a dashing wide-brimmed hat. And Grew, he's happy to wield such a shining, sharp knife."

Jack didn't hear the old man's words. He was still dreaming of the starfish, the one he'd given up for food to the Old Heron. *Just to hear a few stray words,* he thought. The starfish was so beautiful — its phosphorescent glow, the way it moved like a cloud.

Then he heard a meow. "Twitch," Jack said, almost like a question.

"Quiet, puss." It was Bogg's voice.

The next thing Jack knew, they'd slit his throat. He didn't even scream.

————

"CUT OPEN HIS CHEST." THE EXCITEMENT IN THE OLD man's voice was barely contained. He was so close now. *So close...*

Grew took his knife and did as he was told. The knife was sharp, but this kind of work was hard and bloody.

"It'd go faster with an axe," said Willy.

"An axe is too imprecise," said the old man. "We must be careful."

When Grew was finished, Jack's heart was exposed. But it wasn't a heart anymore. It wasn't beating. And it glowed with a faint blue light. It was a strange, oblong kind of thing. An orb.

"That's the one," said the old man.

"But where's his heart?" said Bogg with his sandpaper voice.

The old man smiled as he plucked the orb from out of Jack's cold chest. "The heart of every man is just as you see. A thing made for bargaining."

"So now it's on to the Old Heron?" replied Bogg.

"Yes," hissed the old man. "I want to know my fortune."

Somewhere in the room, a black and white stray mewed.

THE WIND MASTERS

Orlios had been climbing since after breakfast. It was now mid-afternoon, and his fingers ached, but he kept going. Rung after rung, he pulled himself up the ladder.

"Don't pack anything. Just the clothes upon your back," they had said, but Orlios ignored them. He needed his books, his writing utensils, a few extra stockings. He didn't think they'd be too much. But two small volumes of verse, a few leaves of parchment, inkwell and quill, and even three pairs of stockings added up to more weight than he had realized. And to carry them all up the cliff—a cliff that shot up into the clouds—became a Herculean task that Orlios was beginning to regret.

But he was almost to the top. Only one more mile, and soon he would be at the very gates of the heavens.

"Then," he thought, "my real work begins."

But for now he climbed. Rung after rung, with aching fingers, and silent cursing for those extra stockings. Up and up. Hand over hand.

The wood of the ladder was smooth, any roughness or texture worn down by time and use. But the ladder itself was sturdy, the frame holding the rungs with an uncanny firmness.

"How many have ventured this way?" he thought. "The masters, of course. But they are so few. And this ladder is gray and too smooth with wear." Orlios thought about his grandsires, and their grandsires, and about how many generations of men and women had sought to complete this journey only to fail, and to fall. Those that did succeed, those that made the ascent and braved the heavens, they were much fewer. And after their time among the clouds, they would make the journey back down, descend the ladder and then take their position as masters in the city, a revered and sacred position. A rarity.

And Orlios would join their ranks. Just two thousand more feet. Less than a mile now.

Rung over rung. Hand over hand.

He never looked down.

To look down was death. More precisely, it was fear. "Fear is death," that was the saying. To look down would mean Orlios would know fear, and then his hands would clench, and his body would freeze, and his climb would be over.

And death.

No, he never looked down. He kept at it, hand over hand, rung over rung.

The clouds were not what he had expected. The naturalists and stargazers had always claimed that the clouds were gaseous forms of water, foggy concentrations of liquid that coalesced into large masses of ever-changing particles. Orlios had expected to find himself in a dense mist once he had ascended so high. But the clouds were nothing like those grim, swamp-like fogs the men of science had claimed. They were more corporeal than mist, soft and downy like sheep's wool. And they weren't huge masses of cloud either; instead, they were much smaller tufts and patches that floated near one another, but which easily swayed and drifted about, especially when something heavier made its way into their drifting current. What looked like one giant mass to those on the ground was really hundreds of much smaller little masses all floating along lazily in bunches like a herd of dumb sheep. When Orlios climbed up into their sphere, he found they parted for him like delicate lilies floating on the calm surface of a pond.

Up here in the clouds, there was still a wind. Orlios relished it, even though he felt his cheeks becoming raw and chapped with each buffet. But at least there was the cool freshness of it. At least there was new air to breathe, new scents from afar. It made him feel that life had not, in fact, ended. That there was still hope in the world.

He wasn't supposed to be climbing this ladder. It had not been time yet to send up a new prentice. The people were still several years off from needing a newly-minted master. Even as their old one had been bedridden these past twelve years, he could still be counted on, still consulted. But the crisis was beyond his knowledge or skill, much to the old master's shame. He was as baffled as the rest.

It had happened without any warning, and at first, no one even noticed. A morning without a breeze is no strange thing, and for most in the city and surrounding farms, those placid hours were a welcome respite from the ragging storms and cyclones which had wracked the countryside in previous days. Everyone sighed and said, "At last. Now we shall have some peace."

But a morning without wind is one thing; a day without any breeze at all is another thing entirely. In the deep, hot summer it may sometimes feel like there is no wind, but even the most humid, wretched, scorching August day will have some movement. Even if it's only an imperceptible current of new air from the north, or a light whisper from the south, there will always be something: some moment where the air lightens or the leaves of the trees quiver.

But on that first day, there was nothing. The air was as still as a boulder, and as heavy too. When the second day came and still the air did not move, people took notice and complained. But by the fifth day, people began to worry, and then to dread. When a month had gone by, that's when the names appeared.

The Heaviness. The Stillness. The Dead Calm.

And it felt like death. Nothing moved, no tree nor branch nor blade of grass, except when human or beast moved it. The subtle movements of the wind, the invisible hands that gave life to the world were seemingly gone. And so was anything fresh. The air that everyone breathed took on the taste of stale bread, the scent of fetid water. The clouds never came because no wind would move them. And the sky itself was like a great glass plate that had been put over the world to seal it off.

Orlios breathed deeply as he climbed, remembering that

not long ago the air below had caught in his throat like dust. He wasn't sure how the wind could blow up here in the clouds, but down below, the clouds and the wind were gone. Perhaps during his ascent, the Heaviness had disappeared. Perhaps he would reach the top and speak to the masters and find that the crisis had already passed.

But something told him, as his arms ached and his fingers grew more and more calloused, that the Heaviness had not departed. He knew the Dead Calm would not leave so easily.

That's why he'd been chosen. That's why the old master of the city called upon the leaders and elders and had them convene a council; that's why they had called out Orlios's name into the dead stillness of the city square, proclaiming him the new prentice. That's why the old master closed his eyes and winced in pain—knowing his time was over—as he placed the burden upon the young man who kneeled nervously by his bedside. The master would not have given up his post, not have surrendered his authority, if the need wasn't dire. He wouldn't have marked Orlios with the sign of the ladder—three deep slashes across his left bicep—if the crisis was not so terrifying and unsolvable.

No, the Stillness still hung over the people below, Orlios knew. Why the wind blew up here, in the realm of the clouds, near the peak of the mountain, he could not explain, but in his heart, he knew that the wind was still gone from the land that stood in the shadow of the mountain.

Hand over hand, rung over rung. His heart beat faster as he approached the summit. He wondered what he would find. No one had given him any instructions, any clue as to what he would need to do once he had ascended the mountain. Would the masters be waiting for him? Would they already know about the crisis down below? Would they already have an answer?

The ladder curved around the edge of the cliff. Orlios could see nothing but sky and rock and the thick black line that marked the summit of the mountain. When his hands reached the curved handle of the ladder, he decided to look down at last. He was at the top; his head was about to crest over the sheer rock face of the cliff. One look down was all he wanted, to mark the height of his accomplishment and see what the clouds looked like from above. He wasn't afraid anymore; he had made it.

The pack on his back slipped down his right shoulder. Something about the way his body moved when he turned to look down made the weight of the pack shift, and the shoulder strap loosened, and before he could stop it, the strap fell from his arm. He reached out his hand—unthinking—tried to grab the strap, and with that sudden, jerking movement, he felt the other strap slip, and the weight of all his books and writing utensils and extra stockings, all of it dragged the pack down, sliding from his back like water from a duck, and Orlios turned, only one hand and one foot on the ladder, and lunged at the pack, desperate to save it, his free hand and foot waving wildly in the empty air, thousands of feet above the desolate earth. Like gulls drifting on the currents of the air, the parchment papers spread their wings and sailed off into the clouds. Heavy leather tomes dropped like stones cast off from the mountain. And the feather quill floated, a lost feather, plucked from Orlios's own wing, down and down and down.

Orlios watched it all tumble into the thick foam of clouds below, all he had brought on the journey, all he had needed, everything gone.

At first, he didn't realize he was looking down. He didn't even realize that he was swinging from the ladder one-handed. The weightless sensation his arm and leg felt as they swayed in the wind didn't alarm him. He felt light and lithe, a sail caught in a sea-foam gust. But as his heart slowly sank with his pack, and he watched everything that had slipped from his back disappear into specks of nothing, suddenly he realized that he was thousands upon thousands of feet above the ground.

The feeling of nausea came first. Then dizziness. Then dread. Fear came last of all, gripping his throat like a shackle. He tried desperately to grab hold of the ladder with his free hand, but the panic shivering through his body made it hard for his muscles and joints to obey. His fingers splayed out and groped wildly for the hard security of the ladder rung. But the more he struggled, the more he felt his other grip begin to weaken. He was slipping away as surely as his pack had done. Soon he too would be a boulder cast down from the mountain; the wind's invisible hand would hurl him to his doom, a warning to others who dared ascend.

But when the wind blew again, it was not to send Orlios to the halls of death. It was a breath of life, a buoy in a storm-tossed ocean, a wave that carried his sinking body back to the surface. The gust of wind lifted his heavy, falling body, catching the billowing sleeve of his shirt, and casting him back up to catch the ladder. His free hand found the rung, and his fingers curled around the smooth, steady beam. His wayward foot found its step again. He was secure, saved by the movement of the air.

Orlios didn't have much further to go, but he never looked down again. He had known fear, and yet somehow, he had escaped death. The wind itself had saved him. There was no other explanation other than fate had decreed that his mission was sacred, that he must ascend the mountain and find the answers that would save his people. He climbed steadily, calmly. Hand over hand, rung over rung. Until he had reached the top.

And all the while he wondered: *Why me?*

———

THE GROUND WAS LUSH, BLANKETED BY UNDULATING waves of tall grass. All that could be heard was the soft swishing of the wind through the green stalks. The plains stretched forth all the way to the horizon and in every direction. There was no civilization here, only a wilderness of bright emerald and pale yellow.

Orlios was surprised by his exhaustion. It shouldn't have surprised him; after all, he had just climbed thousands of feet into the air, scaling the tallest cliff of the known world. But when his knees buckled and he fell upon the soft turf, his ascent finally at an end, he wanted nothing more than to let his entire body fall to the ground, to rest his head and sleep.

The sky was an overwhelming blue. No clouds were there to soften the sharpness of that blue, to frame it and give it shape. It was simply endless and overwhelming. Orlios had to close his eyes, he had to rest. The waves of grass were like the sounds of flowing water. They sang a lush whisper of sleep, and they told him now was the time to rest. His journey was at an end; he had done well. He could fall into the cold softness of the soil and slumber. He would not need to dream. If there were any masters to be found, he would find them later. He would seek them out, easily. He need only rest and sleep and wait until his eyes could open again.

———

THE GRASSLAND WAS GONE WHEN ORLIOS AWOKE. HE sat up and felt hard, dry pebbles crumble from his cheek. His bed, he suddenly realized, had been rough ground, scattered with dry sand and gravel. Upon waking, he was instantly alert, not drowsy or head-swollen the way a man who has rested well would rouse. He woke as one who was startled from dreams, ready to flee or to fight. The grassy waves had not been a dream or illusion; he remembered them. So why was he now sitting upon barren land, surrounded by rocks and crags, alone in an altogether forbidding place?

Was it the masters?

The ache in his left arm was something new, and he touched the throbbing skin to feel its origin. Under the shirt sleeve, he felt the hot skin and the swollen scabs of the marks the old master had given him. Three slashes. The mark of the ladder. A sign for the masters upon the summit to know that Orlios had been sent. But now they were aching and tender—more tender than when he had first felt the skin slice open from the knife—and they burned with a sharp sting. Orlios knew enough to know that this was the sign of infection. He pulled up his sleeve to see the cuts, looking with revulsion at the puss-filled, sickly yellow of the skin around the wounds, and the blackened scabs that hung from his arm like leeches. His bicep had swelled, and all the flesh was tender and pink from shoulder to elbow.

A breeze blew suddenly-- a tongue of cool, fresh air—and kissed the haggard arm, easing the burning and stinging. Orlios exhaled, not realizing that he had been holding his breath as he gawked at the wound, and then when he sucked in a new breath—a deep draught of the fresh wind—he felt the coolness fill his lungs, calm his nerves, and cleanse his mind. The wind kept blowing, gentle but firm, and the flesh around the gashes grew soft again. The swelling melted and puss began to drain, dripping down Orlios's arm like hot vinegar. Orlios breathed again, and again his lungs were renewed, his muscles revived. And the scabs across his arm flaked away, leaving only pink and soft scars in their place.

Orlios stared wide-eyed at the scars. He felt his arm again. All of the heat and burning was gone. All of the puss had been drained and lay in a drying puddle on the gravel. The infection had lifted, carried away by the wind.

This was impossible. Orlios shook his head and blinked several times. Where had the grasslands gone? Where was he? How was it that moments ago he had been wincing in pain and panicked by infection? And where were the masters?

Even though his lungs were filled with strengthening air, and his heart was grateful for the healing of his arm, Orlios was nevertheless overcome with a terrible dread. This place was not what he had expected. The strangeness, the emptiness, the solitude was wrong. He could feel it. Something was amiss, even as the wind around him tried to buoy his thoughts. It felt as if the breeze was blowing him—but gently, like a lioness nuzzling her cub, urging him along. It was offering to be his guide, to show him where he needed to go.

He decided to follow.

The ground under his feet inclined slightly as he walked. Orlios could feel the slope of the terrain rising; the steady, stoney hills growing higher. As he followed the breeze, it led him deeper into a maze of crags and boulders, and he had to trust the wind. If something was nearby, Orlios feared he wouldn't see it until too late. All he saw was stone, rock, gravel. The wind clipped above his head, too wide and weightless to sink into the crevices through which Orlios now clambered. But it did not abandon him; it carried him forward, picking up strength and force as it ascended, acting as a companion for the lonely prentice.

Orlios wondered if this was the beginning of his training. Is this how the masters welcomed their new acolytes? Perhaps it was a good sign; the wind had extended a friendly hand, taken Orlios under its invisible wing. Perhaps Orlios was being led to the masters even now, those learned ancients who seemed to know all things and decipher all mysteries. Perhaps they had seen him coming, through whatever farseeing magics they possessed, and sent the wind to bring him before their thrones. He hoped he was ready for their tutelage.

THEY SAT UPON THEIR HIGH SEATS, LONG-ROBED AND impassive, gazing upon the skies as if they could see the very currents of the wind. Orlios watched from behind the rocks, careful to stay hidden. Somehow he knew that if the masters saw him, he would be in danger. Why he felt this warning, he could not say. It was like a voice inside him whispered caution.

The masters were not as he expected. They looked as if their skin had been stretched too tightly across their bones, but their eyes were wide and gleaming, heavy with moisture. Their robes hung over their brows, but their faces were not hidden. Orlios almost wished they had been, for their visages were so alike to one another that Orlios thought he was seeing the same face grafted onto a dozen separate bodies. They looked immeasurably old but unnaturally strong, like men made of stone or steel. They held their heads up, looking to the sky for some message or sign. They paid no attention to the young man hidden among the rocks below.

A heavy squall rushed past suddenly, lifting the soles of Orlios's feet, billowing his shirt like a main sail. The rocks, which felt so firm and unshakeable moments before, now rattled. Pebbles and debris swirled around in a frantic dance. The skin on his arms and legs prickled as Orlios clenched his teeth. It was a biting wind, sharp like broken ice.

But the masters seemed not to feel it. They were neither surprised nor shaken by the squall. Orlios watched in disbelief. Opening their mouths wide as if to shout or to sing, the masters swallowed the wild air, drinking the wind like a savory draught. The wind was powerless; it could do nothing but let itself be devoured. Like a worm in the mouth of an owl, the wild air was swallowed by the long-robed masters, their lips curling over the unseen elements, their tongues tasting that which tastes of snow and cloud.

After they had taken their fill of the squall, nothing about their appearance changed, and yet Orlios could see something. They were engorged now with the life and power of the wind. There was something in their eyes, something brighter than human. The masters did not move or speak, but they smiled, all of them at once, like greedy cats. And their eyes celebrated this victory.

As soon as the wind had been swallowed, the squall was dead, and the air upon the peak took on that deadly calm and staleness which Orlios knew all too well. It was the Heaviness. There upon the summit of the highest mountain, within the crags and rocks of that barren place, the Dead Calm came, a shroud and a portend. One by one, the masters lifted their heavy bodies from their high seats and turned from their perch. They disappeared, a slow-moving line of shapeless robes walking beyond the edge of the hill. They took the wind with them, leaving Orlios to sit in the stillness and feel the familiar dread of the motionless air. Would they come again? he wondered. Is that what they do, sit upon their thrones and drink the wind from the heights of the world? Steal that which is not rightfully theirs? Leave the world below to suffocate in its heaviness?

Most who knew Orlios before he'd been chosen prentice would have called him meek; his books and his poetry were a sign of his softness. He loved verse and quiet walks, flowers cut fresh and placed upon a window ledge. He fumbled when he spoke and never once competed in the races or grappling tournaments. But in that moment upon the summit, sitting in the gravel and dirt, weighed down by the unnerving calm and stillness of the world, something hard began to form within him, something Orlios had never felt before. It was hard and hot, and it settled inside his stomach, and grew within his throat, and filled his head with a kind of fire that kindled only one thought. Justice.

He had nothing at hand to use, but Orlios knew that he would strike the masters when he found them. He would crush them, even if he must use his fists or his feet or the barbaric fury of his teeth. He would end their gluttony. If he had not lost his quill, he would have stabbed their necks with it. He would not let them get away with their crimes. The masters, those who had been tasked with serving the world, leading its people through trouble and woe, they had dared to betray their duties, to steal the very thing which they had been consecrated to protect. Orlios felt such irrational, violent wrath that he almost slammed his fist into the jagged rocks nearby. He was full of such anger, he lost all sense of himself. The only thing that mattered was to find the masters and destroy them.

He left his hiding place, walking out into the bright sun and up to the top of the hill, and looking out across the barren landscape, he began to follow the ever-vanishing line of dark robes.

———

THE MASTER'S WATERY EYES DID NOT BLINK. THEY FIXED upon the quivering man and skinned him from top to toe.

"You have tasted a few morsels. I can see it in your face. There is buoyancy. You swallowed the smallest drop and now you have come to swallow more. But how did you find us? How did you know?"

The basalt eyes of the master never wavered; they locked Orlios in their gaze and wouldn't relent. They demanded an answer, and the younger man had no choice but to give it.

"If I had known, I wouldn't have come alone." Orlios wanted to say the words with all the strength and force he had felt earlier, when he witnessed the stealing of the wind. But instead, the sounds that came from his lips were mere whispers. Weak. Within the vaulted ceilings and marbled halls of the great masters, Orlios felt like an intruding worm. The masters stood before him on a raised dais, twelve pillars of dark robe and glistening eyes. Orlios could see the life still coursing through their bodies. Their skin was even more translucent than before, when he first beheld them, and the veins beneath pulsed with vibrant color. Radiating a cold glow, the masters seemed to be something other than human, something primeval.

"You would share the wind? You would let other drink this draught?" cried the eldest master. "Astonishing!"

It took all of Orlios's strength to shake his head. "I've come to throw you from your high places. To take back what is rightfully ours."

"Ah." The watery eyes closed at last. The other robed men nodded.

Orlios felt like screaming, but when he spoke, his voice was steady and low. Calm. "We thought we had done something wrong. We thought the winds had abandoned us."

"The winds do not abandon. The winds do not feel. They are a force of nature." All the masters spoke in unison, as if their voices were united by the tongues of the wind.

"We thought so too," Orlios replied. "Then they disappeared."

The eldest one's face twitched, just slightly. Orlios wondered if the masters had any notion of what their theft had cost. Did they even know that their gluttony had cursed the world below?

"Return the winds!" Orlios said, too desperately. The calm was seeping away, a breath escaping under the window sill.

The cold eyes reflected no warmth. They felt no pity. "How can we return that which is gone? Which is no more? It now lives within us. Only within us."

"That's a lie!" cried Orlios, all his patience and fear gone. "Here, at these heights, the winds still bluster and blow! They saved my life, even. On the ladder. They caught me. Like hands plucking me from certain death. The winds are here!"

All the robed men held their breath, waiting for the air around them to move, for some tongue of wind to lap against their skin, to punish the novice who dared invoke their power. But no wind came. It had fallen silent at Orlios's words. All the masters began to wonder in the silence of their cold hearts: *Why? Why this one?*

Never in all their long years did they imagine that someone would challenge them. Never did they conceive a threat from the mortals who crawled upon the lower earth. For the weak and feeble mortals who scurried upon the earth were like ants to the masters in their high seats. And yet here was a youth—weak and unremarkable—to whom the winds gave some deference.

The heavens above were as dark as a stone bowl, covering the rocky temple with vast emptiness. No stars shone, no clouds lingered. Icy and hard as tempered steel, the sky hung over them and did not move. Waiting. Holding its own breath.

Orlios wished he still had his quills. He would fling the ink into the eyes of the masters and prick their necks, and hope that such punctures would release all the wind they had stolen. He could see it so clearly: the fierce winds would burst forth from the masters' necks, return to the atmosphere, filling the trees with their rustlings, filling the mouths of those crawling upon the lower ground, filling the city with life again. Some part of him was shocked at his boldness, his anger, his desire for action. But some part of him relished it. Is this why he was chosen?

Closing his eyes, Orlios could see it all; he could almost see the wind itself, frost and currents swirling like tendrils through the whole world. He squeezed his eyes until tears ran from the corners, wishing and seeing the wind in the blackness behind his eyelids.

The wind was there, gathering strength. The invisible currents were now visible, as real as tongues of ice. He watched them snake across the backs of his eyelids until they billowed out of sight. They seemed to be inviting him, coaxing him, but he did not know yet to what end.

Orlios clenched his eyes shut even tighter.

His lids were as dark as a stone bowl now, as dark as a sky with no stars. Staring into that blackness, he focused on the taste of the wind in his mouth. Its taste was clearer than water and more dense. More terrible. It had welled up from inside his chest and settled on his tongue. He savored the morsel. He swallowed it again, like a drop of saliva on the lips of a parched man. He tasted it a third time, holding it in his mouth. Waiting.

What would happened if he parted his lips and let the storm rage? What would the masters do then? Would a gale rush forth and topple them? Would a hurricane flatten their temple and release the devoured winds back unto the earth?

Orlios kept his eyes shut, but he opened his mouth.

His ears could hear nothing above the howling din, but his skin felt the chill of frost, the bite of wind. He knew the cyclone ravaged. He felt rocks and thrones topple all around him. And he felt his own body buckle under the force of the vengeful element. He wondered what the masters were thinking, as their bones and bodies were wracked by the winds, destroyed by the same air they had sought to devour and control. He wondered too if his own death might not be in vain. Perhaps, he thought, perhaps all will be set to right.

It was a moment or it was a hundred years, but suddenly Orlios was floating. Like a feather, his body drifted down. Buoyed by the breezes, he descended back to the earth below. At last, he felt the shock in his feet as bones made contact with hard, solid ground. With surprise and alarm, Orlios understood that he was not, in fact, dead.

He smelled the hot air, stagnant and decayed, but still, he did not open his eyes. He kept his vision fixed upon the stone bowl, the vast darkness. He wondered if somewhere scattered about were his books and his quills and his extra stockings. Instead he waited, and realized his mouth was empty.

Orlios felt the weight of a thousand years; he was a young man suddenly made old. He almost collapsed to the ground in exhaustion, but something kept his limbs aloft. Something small but unfettered. Something cool and light. Something that touched his cheek like a bit of frost, a splash of life on a hot day. Something a bit like a breeze. Or a wind.

He opened his eyes and looked down. Death no longer waited for him on the ground, only his own two feet. But something drew his eyes outward, and there he saw around him the patches of forest and field, the familiar countryside outside the city. His city. He watched the trees bend. They were jostled to and fro by an unseen hand, and their leaves waved wildly, like torn rags.

The master smiled. His days as a prentice felt so long ago, but everything had moved so fast since he'd ascended the mountain and swallowed the wind. He was the only master remaining; he shuddered to think what lay atop the plateau now. Not even ruins. Mere rubble, if anything at all. And threads of dark robes. Now, he alone could temper the wind and the rain.

But Orlios had no desire to temper or stall the storm. It was coming at last, and it would not be stilled. The calm was finally over.

A BUSHEL OF BLACKBERRIES &
THE SPIDERS' GOLD

A bigail couldn't wait to taste the blackberries from Mother Haggle's bushel. Swinging her empty basket back and forth, she trotted to market along the gravel path, watching the bees and grasshoppers playing in the tall grass that bordered the way.

It was high summer, Abigail's favorite season. She mostly ignored the bugs that turned the world into their playground this time of year—all the beetles and ants and wasps that plagued her mother's garden—but she did love the honeybees, and the grasshoppers made her laugh, their little wings whirling into buzzsaws and making them leap over everything.

She was getting hot in the mid-morning sun, but soon the village would take her in and give her canopies to rest under and shady stalls in which to take refuge. She loved the busyness of market day. Not only blackberries, which stained her fingers when she plucked them from Mother Haggle's store, but all the wonderful garlands of woven flowers and the exotic fabrics from far-off places that were patterned like a kaleidoscope of colors. She loved the sound of the merchants as they called out for customers, their voices like chiming bells at noontime. Hats and capes and socks and rugs, and all manner of spices that smelled to Abigail like summer must smell in the distant desert kingdoms. She loved it all.

How she wished her mother might come one! To enjoy the scents and sights of the market!

But her mother never came. She was too busy, her fingers chapped and scalded by laundry water and calloused from churning the butter. Her mother's face was always flushed red, like a radish.

"Market day's for the young," her mother would sigh. "For youthful girls to spend their high summer days. Not for old crones like me."

Abigail looked at her mother sometimes, while they were both making the cheese or darning socks, and if she squinted just right, she could see a touch of youthfulness in her mother's well-worn cheeks, and she could imagine how her mother must have looked in younger days.

"You're not so old, Mother," she would say, but her mother just sighed and got back to work.

At first, the bees and the grasshoppers were enough entertainment for Abigail as she crunched her way across the pebbled path with her thin-soled shoes. The village wasn't too far ahead, though all she could see was the endless path and the green fields on either side. The tall grass looked like a parted sea, and Abigail wondered what tiny creatures might be scurrying beneath those tall stalks, or what birds might fly up from the ground with worm or caterpillar in their clever beaks.

The shoes her mother had stitched were motley, stray colors from leftover bits of leather, but Abigail loved them because her mother had made them. The crooked stitches and uneven patchwork were signs of her mother's care. Even though cobbling was not her skill, Abigail's poor mother would do anything for her daughter so that she might have something to cover her feet. For the journey to the market—though not over-long—was still a journey, and Abigail could not walk it barefoot.

She watched her shodden feet march to and fro up the path, beating out a regular rhythm and making a game of it. She started to hum a little tune to the beat, making up silly words to pass the time. It was a glorious day, even if it was over-warm. The rhythm and the song took Abigail into a revelry, stirring her mind with far-off thoughts of distant kingdoms.

That's when she saw the first spider.

Its hairy black body scampered in front of her, darting out from the tall grass and scurrying across to the other side. Abigail wasn't cruel in nature, so she stopped a little and let the tiny thing pass. But then, a few steps later, another spider scurried out and did the same as the last. Abigail stopped and watched it hurry along, and then she started paying better attention to the edges of the path and the place where the gravel met the dirt, and soon she saw dozens of spiders.

They weren't exactly following her, but they weren't not following her either. They gathered together in clumps along the grass's edge, and then every once in a while, one would break off and cross the path. A few times, Abigail was almost certain, two or three of these breakers seemed to be studying her, slowing down on their journey across the gravel to give her the once-over, to study her shoes and her feet.

They weren't particularly nasty spiders. Just the normal kind found in fields and forests. Black and somewhat thick in their legs, but rather on the small side. If Abigail had seen just one, she wouldn't have minded. But the dozens of them all clumped together on either side of her, and their insistence at crossing the path and watching her—

She wasn't too proud to admit that the spiders scared her a little.

She tried to ignore them. The village and the market were almost near, just another half a mile more. In fact, Abigail could see the buildings up ahead, and all the stalls open and bustling in the center square. She felt the pouch of coins on her belt and let their familiar jingle soothe her. Soon she would be tasting the blackberries and tracing her fingers across the smooth silks, too costly for her to buy, but a satisfying dream nevertheless.

Thinking about silks and furs and spiced wines that the vintners sometimes let her taste, Abigail almost missed the golden nugget lying in the path. She had been trying hard to ignore the spiders, to keep them out of her vision, but in doing so, she kept the gold out too. It was only when her foot stepped down on the nugget and felt the hard pebble press into the bottom of her thin-soled shoes, that she stopped and took notice.

"Oh!" she said, startled to find such a treasure simply

lying on the path. That small gold nugget was worth more than all the coins Abigail carried in her pouch.

Who had dropped it, she wondered. Some rich traveler or one of the merchants? If Abigail tried to spend it in the market, would someone find her out and report her to the duke's men? It would be suspicious indeed for a young peasant girl to spend a gold nugget in the market square. But who could she return it to if she didn't know who dropped it?

There was nothing to do but leave it be. Whoever owned it would notice its absence and come back, retracing their steps until they found it.

Abigail wiped a bead of sweat from her forehead and continued on, swallowing a gulp of hot air and wishing for all the world that she had stumbled upon a cup of water instead. The day was monstrously hot now. The market couldn't come soon enough.

But now her eyes were trained to see, and her breath caught in her throat when she saw more gold nuggets, some in the path and some along the side of the gravel amongst the grass. And not only the nuggets, but the spiders too, and they were carrying the gold upon their tiny brown backs. The pieces strewn upon the ground were ones the spiders had dropped, too heavy to carry.

Abigail froze, the sun bearing down on her like an accusing eye, but she couldn't move nor could she think. It was like the world had tilted sideways, and she was going to fall off.

The spiders started to notice her too, and instead of carrying the gold from one side of the path to the other, they started clustering around her feet, dropping gold dust and pebbles of ore right at her toes.

"For me?" said Abigail, astounded. "But I—"

Still, the spiders came and brought her gold.

Something told her this was not the treasure of a rich man, and her stomach rumbled harder than ever when she realized how famished she'd become. Her throat was dry with heat.

What a feast she could get from Mother Haggle...

Abigail closed her eyes and swept the golden pieces into her hand and stuffed them into her coin pouch.

The spiders brought more and more, and the bigger pieces kept tumbling from their backs, but Abigail held up a hand.

"No," she said. "This is too much. They'll grow suspicious. Only a little, please. I'll buy a few more berries, that's all. Even Mother would not believe me. No more, I beg you."

"Your mother is near," she heard a voice whisper. It felt more like a thought in her head than an actual voice, but when it spoke again, she knew it was not her own voice but that of a stranger.

"She is waiting for you."

Abigail whirled around to see who had spoken, but the only things she saw were the familiar things: bees and grasshoppers and gravel and grass.

And the spiders, still busy carrying gold to her feet.

"Did you—?" she started, thinking the impossible. She didn't like spiders, not one bit, but the thought of talking spiders terrified her even more. They dropped more gold at her feet, but it might as well have been cow dung. All she could think was to get away. She had to. She must.

She ran.

Gravel kicked up behind her in a thick, smokey cloud, and whether the spiders followed or not, Abigail didn't know. She never looked back, only ran towards the town and the market stalls and what she hoped would be safety.

Panting and sweating through her linen dress, she knew she must have looked awful, but now that the noise and bustle of people surrounded her, she felt more at ease. It was true, some folks gave her strange looks as she stood there gulping for air in the hot sun, and she did run like a devil from the path into the market square, but now that she was in the town, away from the tall grass and the insects and most of all the spiders, she felt much better about things.

She spotted Mother Haggle soon enough, the old woman's stall fronted by bushel upon bushel of berries and fruit and the first fine grapes of the season.

Abigail only had eyes for blackberries.

She trotted over to the stall and beamed at the sight of the purple-black berries swelled with juice and the taste of summer. She had enough gold pebbles to buy not only the bushel but every berry in the stall, but Abigail hesitated to take the gold out. A taint lingered on the ore, and her thoughts were still disturbed by that strange voice.

"What about you?"

Having finished with her previous customer, Mother Haggle shuffled her hunch-backed body over to Abigail. Her voice was sharp and wary, and she raised a distrusting eyebrow at Abigail. "Eh? Cat got your tongue, you little devil?"

The tone of Mother Haggle's voice made Abigail blush and step back. She had never spoken to Abigail that way before, and the look in her eyes made Abigail think the old woman didn't recognize her. She felt like a peeled grape under the gaze of those suspicious, watery eyes.

"Away with you, then!" Mother Haggle said, flapping her fleshy hand up and down like she was shooing a cat. "None of your kind at an honest woman's stall!"

"But, Mother Haggle—" Abigail began.

"I'll call the constable, I will!"

"It's me, Abigail Merritt!"

"A liar too! Be gone!" She practically shoved Abigail away. "I know who you are! Can't fool this Haggle's eyes!"

"But—"

"Away!"

Sweat was pouring down the back of Abigail's neck, drenching her upper undergarments so that they stuck to her hot skin like a second flesh. All she could do was back away from the stall and find another canopy to settle under.

But as she stood in the midst of the square, the dark faces and eyeing looks of passersby only increased, and at every stall, scowling merchants greeted her. They shook their heads and warned her off, and she didn't know why.

Did they know about the gold? Did they think she had stolen it? But how could they? It was too impossible.

She found a narrow alley off the main drag of the marketplace. The sun was at the wrong angle to penetrate past the stone walls of the buildings on either side, but the heat was no better here than in the square. It was stifling. Abigail wiped her brow again, and then with trembling hands, took out her pouch and undid the drawstring.

The gold inside shimmered even in the half-shadows. She overturned the pouch and down came the gold alongside the coins from her mother, all of it clattering across the cobblestones.

Oh, how she wished her mother had come to market! If her mother was here, no one would scowl or suspect. Her mother could explain everything to these narrow, distrustful people.

"Your mother's here," came a whispered reply.

"Where?" Abigail said. She spun around in the cramped lane to see who had spoken. Some boy from the village, perhaps. Come to taunt her.

But no boy had spoken.

"She's here. Follow us."

The glint of the gold caught her eye. She looked down and saw them. The spiders were creeping along the cobblestone, coming from all the dark corners of the walls, circling the gold pieces and coins on the ground.

"This is her treasure," the spiders said, for now Abigail was certain they were whispering to her. Not with mouths—she wasn't even sure spiders had proper mouths—but with their minds. Their voices creeped inside her head like they creeped along the ground, stealthy and swift.

"My mother has no treasure," replied Abigail. "If she did, do you think we'd live in our little cottage on the outskirts of this nowhere village? My mother deserves a treasure, it's true. For all the work she does, all the hardships she's endured. But you're as wrong as those people out there in the square. I didn't steal this treasure, and it's not my mother's, and I wish you'd all leave me alone!"

This last bit she shouted, and then she looked up the lane to see if anyone had heard her. But to the people in the market square, she was as unseen as these spiders hiding in the shadows.

"Your true mother," they hissed.

Abigail's body, so hot and sweaty, was suddenly chilled. It was not normal for spiders to speak into one's head, and it wasn't normal for them to carry golden nuggets upon their back. But these things Abigail could somehow rationalize. They were happening to her, after all, so she had to accept them.

But a true mother? What did that mean? What could it mean?

Her blood thickened with fear. She didn't know why, but it terrified her. She had only one mother, the woman she loved so dearly, who had raised her all her life. That was her true mother.

"Follow," said the spiders. "Follow, for your mother calls, and her words must be answered."

Abigail managed to shake her head. "I will not. I'm going home."

"You can't go back there."

"Yes, I can."

All Abigail could think about now was her home, her dear mother with weary eyes but a warm smile. She would find her at her spinning wheel in the corner, fingers gently feeding the wool into the machine, and she would tell

Abigail to fill the kettle, for soon she would break from her work and they'd have tea. Abigail could smell the fibers of the wool, and she could hear the whistle of the kettle. The heavy iron smell of the hot stove too. And the chicory for the tea.

"I will, in fact," she told the spiders and started walking back into the square.

But the hulking, scowling figure of the constable was nosing his way toward the narrow lane, searching her out. He hadn't spotted her yet, but if she stayed much longer, he would. And what then?

Abigail turned behind to see where the lane went, but to her surprise, a towering pile of broken crockery and busted wagon wheels and scraps of wood and stone, and even someone's iron cook stove were all stacked on top of each other to make a barrier that blocked her way.

She knew instantly that the pile of junk had appeared out of nowhere, but the spiders gathered around her feet like pieces of soot, and she could feel a strange *something* seep through her skin.

Magic.

The gold pebbles at her feet mocked her.

"I'll climb my way out," she said, striding over to the mountainous pile. "You can't stop me."

"This way. Come."

She stopped dead in her tracks. To her left, where had once been stone, was now a door in the wall, a black nothingness that shimmered slightly, like a shadow on a hot day.

"Pick up the gold and follow. Your mother is waiting."

"No," said Abigail, but the word was barely a whisper and died on her lips even as she said it.

The constable was coming. She could hear his shouts and feel the redness of his puffy face, even though she wasn't looking at him. His yells blew steamy smoke down the alley, and his words were all garbled, like words in a dream.

The spiders were crawling up her legs, carrying the gold back into her leather pouch. They drove her into the shadows. She had no choice.

The portal in the wall swallowed her, and the last thing she heard was the incomprehensible anger of the constable's shouts.

The darkness was immeasurably cold. Every bead of sweat on her skin froze into a sheen of frost, and Abigail's teeth chattered. Darkness engulfed her. The absence of light was a living organ pulsing around her, sucking in every thought of day or sun or even stars, until the only thing that remained was darkness, an all-encompassing darkness, as cold as the farthest reaches of space.

Abigail remembered winter skies at night, when the stars seemed to fire brightest. Those beautiful pricks of light that dazzled like fire. She had loved those lights, a map of alien wonder to guide travelers and seekers and sailors on their way.

Now she wondered if there was a place beyond the stars, a place where no light ever shined. An utter darkness. For this blackness was such a place, and she was trapped in it.

Like the cloudy nights when she was little, when the cottage was cold and the fire in the hearth was so low that it was barely an ember, and Abigail would stare up at the ceiling and see only darkness and hear a faint, wheezing breath—her mother's breath—but it would frighten her because it didn't sound like her mother but like a starved animal or a ghost. Those nights were like this moment, and this moment was as lonely and empty as anything Abigail had ever felt.

"Child." The voice was thin as a knife. "Child, you came."

She wanted to say, *Don't call me child*, but the darkness dampened every nerve in her throat and her tongue too. She wondered if this was what the grave felt like, all the dark earth squeezing around. A void. An emptiness.

Then—

Out of that emptiness, a small, faint glow began to stir. It grew to the size of a skull: an old woman's face, wizened and lined with cracks.

"No," Abigail's voice whispered. "No."

She was hunched and crouched over a spinning wheel, wearing the same kerchief she always wore. She smiled her smile, but it was toothless.

"No."

She spun the thread and clicked her feet against the pedal, and nodded at Abigail.

"Child," she said, that thin, reedy voice.

"No, you're not her."

"I am. All your life, child. Come and give Mother a kiss upon the cheek."

"No."

"Willful child. We shall teach you."

The spiders were crawling all over Abigail now. She wanted to jump out of her skin.

"Give me my gold, daughter dear. Bring it near so I may count it. We've grown ever so poor. I rely upon you, my child, to go to market and find our fortune."

Abigail had no will of her own. The spiders moved her like a marionette, like a dead fly they were carrying to supper. She found herself face to face with the wizened crone, the woman in her mother's kerchief. When she was up close, she saw the woman had no eyes. Just empty sockets. Her skin was thin and brittle as parchment. Every inch of her stank of death.

"Ah, yes. There it is. The gold." The crone stopped spinning and stuck out a bony hand.

Abigail recoiled, for the hand was real bone. A skeletal hand, draped in threads of thin brown skin.

But the spiders made her open the pouch and drop the gold into the waiting palm.

The old crone's face pinched itself into a smile.

"More," she said, raw as January. "More, my child. Gather it all up and free me from this place. Then we shall go on the road together. You and I, mother and daughter."

Abigail was repulsed by the woman, and she wanted to rear back and run. If nothing else, she wanted to protest. She thought of her dear, sweet mother—her real mother—and hated this twisted imitation.

But she neither ran nor resisted. She swallowed hard and felt the cold drop down into her like a stone.

"I shall," she answered. "But call off these creatures." She batted away an armful of spiders. "I can do it on my own."

The wind sucked through the crone's teeth. "My daughter!" she cried. "At last!"

Then the wind was howling all around Abigail, a terrible cyclone, lifting her skirt and stinging her eyes. And the darkness was back again, blacker than pitch. Abigail felt weightless and formless, and she didn't miss seeing the crone, but she did miss the light. She even missed the spiders, for she couldn't tell if her skin was real or not without their touch upon her. She was a ghost now, a bodiless thing. All darkness and wind and chill.

The narrow lane was humid when she returned, standing where she had stood when the constable was coming for her. Her skin was sweating already, and sticky, and she ran her fingers across her forehead to wipe away the moisture. She knew she must look a fright, and it gave her an ache to think what her mother would say. It was so hot: a drenching, oppressive heat that weighed her down like sludge.

But it was not the sun's heat, for the sun was gone. It was night but not night, a twilight as purple as blackberries. And yet the heat was hotter than ever, a furnace of invisible fire that blazed all around her.

The lane was empty and dark, and when she looked to the square, she thought at first that it was empty too. But it was only the twilight that obscured things. For when she looked again, she saw that the stalls were still up, and shadowy figures stood beneath the canopies.

The figure of Mother Haggle was obvious. Like a round, ripe grape, her body swayed unnaturally in the darkness, hovering over the barrels of fruit. Abigail's pouch was empty now, and bitterness stung her throat. Why, oh why, had she picked up that gold! All for an extra mouthfuls of berries!

Her stomach hungered like she hadn't eaten in days. No money in her pouch, but perhaps in this darkness, she could palm a few morsels. It was wrong, of course, but when a person starved, even thievery was permitted.

Abigail swallowed the humid air, screwed up her courage, and stepped into the square. None of the shadowy figures moved. They were as still as the posts that framed them.

Straight to Mother Haggle, Abigail moved like a breath of wind. She would bargain with the woman to distract her. Then, with her stomach fed, she could scour the path for more gold. More gold for—

As she walked toward the stall, Abigail knew this place was unnatural, that the twilight and the heat and the corpse-like merchants were all wrong, but her hunger was such that it made all else vanish, even the weirdness of the scene. Her tongue ached for the sweetness and tart of the blackberries.

"Mother Haggle," she called as brightly as she could. "My own mother bids me buy your fruit!"

Mother Haggle's eyes were deep pools of midnight. She opened her mouth but no sound came out. Just empty eyes and gaping mouth.

Abigail yelped.

Mother Haggle's hands moved back and forth, displaying her goods, but she moved like an automaton, thoughtless and mechanical. Abigail took a step back and looked around the square again. All the shadowy figures were thus, moving in jerky, repetitive movements like machines. It was a pantomime, a fake.

The heat grew hotter and the twilight darker.

Inside the barrels of blackberries, something glinted in the half-light.

"Gold…" Abigail's hand went forward instinctually, reaching for the shining nuggets. "Mother says I may have some," she said. When her hand plunged into the dark pond of berries, she grabbed both gold and fruit, but when her stained fingers emerged, a flash of bone-white caught her eye.

A skeleton hand.

She flinched, dropped the gold and berries, and cried out.

But when she looked again, her hand was quite normal. Stained with juice, but flesh and blood. Mother Haggle took no notice, only stood gaping with her mouth wide and eyes black.

When Abigail stooped to pick up the gold, she saw the spiders lingering, keeping watch like guards. It annoyed her to think they'd been sent. Wasn't she a good daughter? Obedient and true. She would prove it. She would show these creatures how loyal she could be.

The berries were rotten. Looking again at the barrel, she saw that they were all of them rotten.

Every piece of fruit at Mother Haggle's stall was over-ripe and crawling with decay. Those fresh morsels from this afternoon had aged a week or more.

The humidity, Abigail thought, but she couldn't convince herself.

"My mother thanks you," she heard herself saying. She couldn't help it. The words came out unbidden. Her hands, too, scooped back into the barrels and plucked out all the gold. No more skeleton hands, but with every nugget she gathered, Abigail knew how pleased her mother would be and grew eager to bring the treasure home.

Home.

Not to her mother, no. Not to her home either, that terrible dark place.

But she wanted to go there, wanted to see Mother again. Yes, Mother would be pleased. She would be free. Soon, soon. How happy Mother would be!

Abigail wished her mother could be with her. How fine she would look in that marketplace! She was not so old. Not so old at all.

There was more gold to gather, so Abigail gathered it. After Mother Haggle's stall, she went to the silk merchant, then to the spice traders, and after that, to the craftsmen to see what treasures they could give. All of them were speechless, made no fuss, their eyes like puddles of black mud. They opened their mouths and wordlessly bid Abigail to take her due.

For they had stolen this gold. Thieves. The whole lot of them. Abigail felt righteous as she gathered up her mother's riches. These belonged to Mother, and soon they would free her.

Her pouch swelled by the end of her shopping, though her basket was empty. The spiders danced around her shodden feet like children on holiday. She had gold in that pouch, and it felt good to know that soon she would be going home.

The hotness of the twilight was beginning to melt even

the wax in the candlemaker's shop, but he didn't seem to mind. His mouth stood gaping and no sound came out, his face as still as the moon.

Abigail waved to him and the others, a smile across her face.

The second time around, the darkness was not so frightening. When she went to Mother again, she relished the darkness, letting it cover her like a mantle.

"There is one more," her mother said, twirling a thread of yarn around her bony finger. "A peasant woman outside the village. She has my gold too. Get it for me and we shall be free."

All of Abigail's confidence fled. She could feel the spiders drawing closer, accusing her. A peasant woman outside the village? Did she have a daughter too?

"I—"

"You will," hissed the voice of Mother. "The last of my gold."

"She doesn't, though," Abigail said, trying to recall a memory. A sweeter face at the spinning wheel. "She has nothing. Not a drop of gold."

"She does!" said Mother, the mask slipping. Bones flashed through paper-thin skin. Decay ran rampant through the air. "And you will bring it back to me."

The spiders followed Abigail as she left the darkness and the market square. They followed her as she made her way down the gravel path again. The grass waved eerily in the twilight, like fur on the back of some terrible beast. And the sky was dim. No moon that Abigail could see. Was it behind a cloud, or gone entirely?

The spiders followed her until the village was out of sight and the world was only tall grass and gravel. Every sound made Abigail jump; the waving of the grass made her flesh crawl. She was glad that the grasshoppers and bees were gone. She was almost glad that the crickets made no sound.

The little cottage was a black spot against the prairie. Mother's voice creeped through her head.

The last of my gold.

But that other face lingered, laying itself atop Mother's withered face like a piece of gossamer. That other face was kind. It was not covetous like Mother's.

Still, the gold. Abigail could feel her fingers itching to grab it.

"My mother bids me—" She stopped. "My mother."

"Who are you?" The voice was frail, frightened.

The spiders crawled into the cottage. There was a spark. A candle lighted. Abigail saw the face—the gentle face, the worried face—and she recoiled.

"Who are you?" the woman said again.

"The daughter of a queen," Abigail replied with words that were not her own.

"And why should the daughter of a queen disturb an old widow?"

The gold, of course. Mother had said. The last of the gold and then freedom.

"You have something that belongs to her," Abigail answered.

"I have very little. Only a daughter to keep me from starving."

A daughter. The words were like a strong tonic, and

Abigail couldn't help herself. She cried out for joy and rushed into the cottage.

But she stopped when she saw the woman's face. It was staring at her in fright. A terror-stricken face. The woman's body trembled as she sat in the rocking chair holding the small candle. Abigail thought the candle might drop because that trembling.

"Please," the old woman said, "please don't hurt me." Her eyes darted around the room, the faint light from the candle barely illuminating anything. But she could see the spiders. They crawled over the floor, and the rug by the hearth, and the old woman's stockinged feet.

"Get out!" Abigail commanded the spiders, and at first they stopped, but then they didn't leave. Instead, they crowded around Abigail's shodden feet, the shoes her mother had stitched for her. They covered her feet in darkness.

"I have nothing that could belong to a queen," the old woman sobbed again. "Nothing."

"Mother," said Abigail, "don't you know me?"

The woman shivered. "What are you saying? My daughter has gone to market and not returned. That was a year ago and a day."

"A year ago and and a day?"

"Who are you?"

"Your daughter."

The woman turned her face away. "Please don't hurt me."

"I would never!"

"I have nothing you could want." She was sobbing now. "My only treasure is gone."

"I'm right here, Mother. Right here." Abigail wanted to move towards the woman, but the spiders had covered her feet, and like tar they had stuck her in place.

"You are the daughter of a queen. She must be terrible indeed to send such a daughter."

Abigail couldn't move her feet, but she reached out her arms, her hands still holding the heavy pouch of gold and the empty basket. In horror, she saw skeletal hands and arms stretched forth.

"I'm a poor widow," the old woman said again. "Don't hurt me."

"You are my mother!" Abigail kept reaching, trying to ignore her fleshless limbs. "I've come home."

"Please, please," the woman begged. "Nothing here. There's nothing."

"Gold," the spiders hissed. "The gold is hidden. Find it."

"There is no gold," said Abigail. "I know there's not. This is my home."

"Gold," insisted the spiders. "The last of the gold."

The spiders scurried off her feet, releasing her. They lingered nearby, but Abigail could now move. And yet she did not move towards the woman in the rocking chair. She held up her hands and forced herself to look.

The flesh was all gone, the clothing turned to rags, and all her bones gleamed as white as freshly polished porcelain. She looked down at her feet. Her shoes were in tatters, the bones exposed. She trembled. Her bones rattled, but she dropped the basket and felt her face. It didn't surprise her, but it frightened her nonetheless.

Bone. All bone. Only her hair remained: thin and wispy

like shreds of spider webbing. She realized now that she was neither hot nor cold. That the air within the cottage was as insubstantial as the air without.

She stepped back. Her poor mother. What had she brought to this place? What terrors had she inflicted?

"The gold," the spiders said again, chittering their many legs upon the floorboards.

"She has none," Abigail said. "Mother was mistaken." She knelt down in agony and fumbled in the dark, looking for the basket she had dropped.

"She is never mistaken."

"This time," said Abigail, feeling around with her bony fingers, "she is. She'll have to wait a little longer."

"And you too," said the spiders. "You will not be free until the queen is free."

"Yes," said Abigail, "I know that now. But she is mistaken."

"She is never mistaken."

As they left the cottage, Abigail heard the heavy sobs of the old widow catch on something. There was silence and then an outcry, and then the candle went out.

Abigail would have smiled if she'd still had flesh.

"Here is your gold, Mother." Abigail stepped into the shadow-dark and held out the empty pouch to the woman at the spinning wheel. Abigail was no longer shocked by the skeletal hand that operated at her command. She had grown used to herself.

"Now," hissed the decaying queen, "we shall both of us be free."

"We shall. And first thing I will do is take you to market. You deserve to go."

"Indeed. I have not seen the sky in a thousand years."

"You deserve to see the sky."

They stepped out of the darkness, through the door in the wall, and into the marketplace. The sky was there, still twilight and purple, and Abigail watched the spiders crawl over every inch of cobblestone. The stalls were empty. No shadows or shades. And the place smelled of decay. A thousand years perhaps or none, but the market square was empty and bereft, nothing to buy nor to sell nor to steal.

"Here we are, Mother. I've always longed for you to see it."

But the queen shrank back. She was caught in the darkness, the hem of her rotten gown was cinched to the shadows.

"The gold," she cried, holding the empty pouch upside down. "Where is the gold?"

"Isn't it there?" said Abigail. "I thought for sure it was there."

"You are mistaken!" The old woman's scream was a winter wind.

"Am I? Then we are both mistaken. It happens, I suppose. Thinking something is there when it is not. Thinking someone is your daughter when she most surely is not."

"But the gold! The spiders said!"

"Perhaps they were mistaken too."

"My daughter!"

"I'm afraid not. But at least you got to see the market. And the sky. One last time."

The darkness sucked them back into itself, the queen back into her tomb, and Abigail too. She would not be free, she knew that now. The utter dark entombed them both.

When the spiders spoke again, she could remember nothing but the cold.

"We thought you were she," they whispered. "She always walked that path, and her mother moaned and moaned to see her again. We thought you might be—"

"I was she, and I am now."

"No, that was too many ages ago," the spiders answered. "We were wrong. Mistaken. Utterly mistaken."

"You were not. It was many ages ago, but Mother's not so old. Not so old at all. And she's been waiting, hasn't she?"

"Waiting to be free."

"Yes, but I'm afraid she'll have to keep waiting."

"Until another daughter comes along," hissed the spiders.

"Another fool, you mean. But there's no more gold to catch her with, is there? That much, I know."

She could not remember the sun, nor the warmth of summer, but she could remember the gold.

It had been left on the outskirts of town. In the cottage of a poor widow. Dropped from a coin pouch into an empty basket.

A basket meant for blackberries.

SALT KISSES

Aoife knew she was adopted and never tired of telling her parents so.

"You're not adopted," her mother would sigh, pushing an auburn hair from her tired forehead. "I think I would know."

But Aoife ignored these obvious protestations, jutting her chin in defiance of what her mother had said.

Her mother was a liar, that much was plain. It was clear to anyone that Aoife could not be the daughter of this woman. Her mother hardly ever cried or looked off into the distance; she never felt the lure of the horizon and what must lay over it. Her mother's horizon was the edge of the threadbare rug, the sea-salt grime on the window panes, the cooking pot that always needed scrubbing.

Aoife was the daughter of the sea. Her mother was all dry land.

"You're getting on my nerves," Mother would reply and then hand Aoife a broom.

Their shabby tin house was always letting in the draft

and the pungent, salty stench of rotten seaweed and fish from the docks. It took Aoife's mother most of the daylight hours to drive out the sea smells. A waste of time, really. They'd just come back inside the next day. Aoife claimed she liked those smells anyway. The lure of the sea, she'd say.

"Try the lure of the front stoop," Mother would reply. "It needs sweeping."

Aoife would scowl, snatch the broom away, and stomp outside. She refused to sweep, staring instead over the thatched and shingled roofs of their street to the tall masts of the ships beyond. Like flags calling her home, their sails billowed as they set off into the blue-gray water.

"You shouldn't talk that way to Mother," Aoife's older sister, Ellen, would lecture. Tall and lithe, Ellen might have been beautiful if her oval-shaped face hadn't gotten scarred from the pox. "Your words are like wounds. They cut her to the heart."

"Don't be such a stuffy prim," Aoife would hiss back. "It's clear as day I'm not her daughter."

The two girls were as opposite as could be. Ellen was quiet, always proper, never bold. Aoife raged like a squall anytime she didn't get her way. While Ellen did all she could to help their family—taking work in taverns or sewing nets with the old women in town—Aoife spent most of her time by the docks and the rocky shoreline, daydreaming.

"You'll be the death of her, Aoife. Is that what you want?"

"What do I care? She's been a wet nurse, nothing more."

These arguments were the only time Ellen showed any strong emotions; most of the time she was measured and demure. But when Aoife took after their mother like this,

Ellen revealed a wave of steaming hot anger that could boil the clothes clean. It was clear what Ellen thought of her sister. Aoife was an ungrateful, wicked brat, undeserving of the great sacrifices and affections their parents showered upon her.

Aoife, for her part, thought Ellen was an insufferable prig.

The weather had been coming for days, but Aoife paid no mind. She could withstand a storm, any storm, for she was born of the sea and had no reason to fear.

"Get home, child!" the grizzled men tying up boats would call. "Storm's a'coming!"

Aoife didn't care. *Let the storm take me,* she thought. Anything was better than life in this salt-dried, rock-hewn village.

The trouble started at school, in the yard before the morning bell. The girls were swarming. Aoife never gave them any courtesy, but today was different. Today, she had the audacity to ignore them completely. She was deep in a daydream, wondering about the very depths of the sea. She saw the eye of a giant squid and didn't notice Catherine O'Connor calling her name.

"Heard a rumor said your feet are covered in scales!"

Aoife didn't reply—not out of rudeness or even shame— but simply because she was swimming in choppy waters with the selkies. Plugged with salt water, Aoife's ears couldn't hear the Catherine O'Connors of the world.

"Why don't you go jump in the sea!" Catherine yelled.

"Drown yourself and save us from having to look at you!" the other girls called out.

Laughter, tart and sharp. Laughter ringing in Aoife's ears, even through the deep waters. Laughter that shook the daydream out like sand from a shell.

The squall raged then and stopped Catherine O'Connor's laughing. Aoife, unfortunately, got sent home by the schoolmaster.

"There'll be your salt kisses again," her father teased when she got home and recounted the injustice done to her. "Daughter of the sea."

"Salt kisses?" Aoife shoved a lock of hair behind her ear.

"Aye, your tears. As salty as the brine on the boat hull. They kiss your face to soothe ye. The sea being your natural parent, o' course."

Aoife didn't think it fair that her father teased her while she was crying. Her parents never showed any tears. They were as dry as bones. Another reason why they weren't her family.

"What did the girls say?" her mother asked, trying to be gentle.

"They asked about her feet," Ellen answered when Aoife refused.

Mother scoffed. "No shame in that. Isn't your fault you had the pox." She said it to Aoife, but her eyes glanced at Ellen.

"It's not from the pox!" Aoife raged. "I've told you! They're—"

"Hush now," Mother said, standing up and going back to the stove. "I'll have no more of that."

Aoife knew it bothered her mother when she mentioned

her true parentage, when she insisted on speaking the truth. But Aoife wasn't going to back down.

"You have no claim on me!" Aoife cried. "I am not your daughter!"

"Aoife, you shouldn't now," her father began, but his words were too weak. As usual.

"Hush." Her mother didn't even turn around. She turned the handle of the spoon in the pot. "Set the table, why don't you? Be useful while you scream."

Aoife grunted and stamped her foot, and before she could even think, she was out of the house. She barely noticed the gathering clouds or the wetness in the air. When she stood by the docks, the old men tying their boats gave her grim looks.

"Be off, young one!" they called to her. "Can't you see what's coming?"

Aoife stared at the waves coming in, all choppy and gray. The sea was cold. She searched the depths for some sign of life, for something to welcome her, but nothing came. In the distance, boats could be seen coming in, trying to get to shore before the worst of the wind howled.

Sitting on the peer, Aoife put her foot across her leg and started unfastening the shoelaces. The shoe came off then the stocking. Her bare foot was exposed to the salty air.

"These are my true feet," she said defiantly.

The skin was dappled with gray spots in a pattern that resembled fish scales. To Aoife, these spots were the remnants of her oceanic origin. They were her body's way of regaining its birthright. They were decidedly *not* scars from the pox.

She thought of how her feet must have been when she

was born. Like the fins of a fish, they must have glimmered. Silver and shimmery, they must have reflected all the colors of the rainbow when the light streamed down through the water.

Now they were a drab gray. Dried out by too much time on land. Aoife wondered if she should dip them into the salt water.

Rain started to sprinkle, blurring the gap between the sea and the sky. Everything was a hazy gray. Aoife stood on the peer, bare feet soaking in the rain. The waves rolled higher and higher as the wind pushed them into crashing swells. The fishermen who had been coming into shore as fast as they could were gone now, hidden somewhere behind the waves and rain or else lucky enough to have reached the docks further down the coast.

Aoife put her face to the stinging rain and looked out as far as she could. Her own tears mixed with the sky's. *This is my home,* she thought. *My fierce, endless, wild home!*

How could her father have given all this up and sold his boat? How could her mother have settled for hanging other peoples' dingy washings and scrubbing floors? The answer was clear. They were not her parents. Her feet were a sign... She belonged to the sea...

"Aoife!" It was Ellen, coming up the road, heading toward the peer. She was wrapped in an old shawl, one of Mother's dark blue ones, knitted on winter nights when the wind bit at the door. It made Ellen look like a banshee, her long, oval face peeking through the dark shawl, her pocked cheeks all sunken by the storm's shadows. "Come away from there!"

The sound of her sister's voice startled her. Aoife turned, her bare feet slipping on the mucky wood, her balance lost.

"Aoife!"

The water hit Aoife's body with a sharp force, and before she knew what was happening, she was submerged. It was like a block of ice had formed all around her. The water was so cold it burned her skin. She had but one thought: *I am drowning.*

All ideas about being born of the sea vanished. For Aoife, water now meant death. She struggled to find her way up to the surface, but every way she went led further into the depths. Her lungs started to burn even as her muscles weakened. Everything was so cold, so dark. Her pockmarked feet couldn't help her. They didn't rescue her or transform into fins or do any of the other things she had dreamed of. A terrifying thought overcame her, like a voice calling from the depths.

Stop moving. Stop fighting. Just sink.

Her long red hair drifted around her like seaweed. The storm waves rocked her body back and forth like a baby in a cradle. She had never given up before, but something about it felt effortless, as if it were the most natural thing in the world to let the waves and the water take her down, down, down. It felt good to give in, to let go.

Ellen's hands grabbed her under the arms and yanked her up. With more strength than Aoife realized her willowy sister had, Ellen pulled her to the surface. Gasping and sputtering, Ellen pulled Aoife close to her in a tight embrace.

"Can you swim?" she cried over the sound of the pouring rain.

Spitting water out of her throat, Aoife could barely talk. She wanted to nod her head "yes," to be strong again and swim to shore, but she couldn't. She had no strength left.

"Hold on!" Ellen commanded then hoisted Aoife onto her back. She tried to swim and carry Aoife at the same time, but the weight was too much. The sea began to claim them both. "Aoife, I can't!" Ellen's voice was panicked. She started to struggle against the pull of the waves, started to sink too. Aoife closed her eyes and thought again of how easy it would be to stop fighting.

"Ahoy! We're comin' for ye, girls!" The grizzled voice of the fisherman could be heard high above the din of the storm. His was a voice that had wailed over many a squall. The boat rocked and crashed its way over the choppy waters until it came close enough for the crew to throw out a net.

When the net splashed into the water, something awoke in Aoife. Fury seized her. Fury against the storm, against the waves, against the sea that wanted to sink her. She was resurrected out of the dark waters, eyes ablaze. Entwining her fingers into the netting, she began to swim again. They heaved her over and up and pulled her onto the boat.

But when they flung the net out again for Ellen, their faces grimaced. The girl was gone.

Aoife didn't know what was happening. She heard voices shouting into the wind, but she couldn't make out what they said. All she knew was there was a heavy jacket suddenly draped over her shoulders, and she was shivering, and she wanted to sink into the musty-smelling jacket and go to sleep. But she heard the shouting, and the rain battering down onto the fishing boat's deck, and she wondered where Ellen was, and why she wasn't sitting there next to her, wrapped in the jacket too.

"We lost her." She heard someone say it. It sounded like it came from within her head, but it must have come from one of the men. It was so soft, though... So near...

Aoife didn't remember much after the boat started in toward shore. She was too cold, too tired to think or hear properly. There were words said above the din, grim faces peering out from beneath soaked caps, but nothing felt real. Aoife simply sank into the heavy jacket and waited. She didn't care how weak it made her feel: She wanted her mother.

———

THE HOUSE HAD TURNED QUIET. NO ONE SPOKE anymore.

Aoife wished her mother or father would speak, would yell or blame or cry out to heaven. Instead, they said nothing. It was like Aoife had turned invisible. As if two daughters had drowned in the sea instead of one.

She had no right to complain, though. Aoife hardly spoke herself.

In the schoolyard, she had lost her saltiness. Her stormy squalls had dried up. When the other children passed by, they avoided her, casting furtive glances at her sad figure: a piece of driftwood cast out of the sea. There were no more taunts or teases from the Catherine O'Connors of the world. Only whispers and unwelcome pity.

At first Aoife said nothing. She stayed quiet in the house

and at school and wherever she went. She was afraid to speak for fear that tears would come. She no longer wanted to feel the sting of salt kisses or anything else.

After three weeks of such silence, Aoife came home from school one day and found the kitchen empty. She half-expected Ellen to be there stoking the fire or helping Mother mend some nets, but the house was dark with late-afternoon shadows instead.

Aoife didn't bother to light the lamps, nor rekindle the cold stove. Wherever her mother might be, Aoife didn't know, but she picked up a broom and tried to ignore the silence as best she could. She moved the handle distractedly, barely looking at the trails of dust she shuffled back and forth.

The front door creaked on its hinges and then stopped. Aoife froze, broom in mid-sweep. She expected her mother to come in, and the thought of it made her body clench. They never fought anymore, not since that day... but her mother's silence was worse than any fight. It was an accusation. A judgment. And Aoife knew her guilt.

Instead of her mother, fingers scratched the wood and an old voice croaked after them.

"Mari?" said the voice, like rusted hinges.

"She's not home," Aoife answered back, "she's—"

The door swung open. A hunched woman wearing a faded red robe shuffled into the room. She wore a silken scarf in motley colors over her head, framing her sunken face and making her eyes and nose stand out. Her eyes were wide and unblinking like an owl's; her nose, bulbous like a radish and just as red. Her cheeks too, though hollow, were tinged crimson. Father had said red cheeks and nose were a sign of those who took too much drink and didn't know when to stop.

The old woman tottered closer, and Aoife stepped back, the broom held in front of her like a quarterstaff.

"I ain't here to hurt ye, dear," said the woman. "I'm looking for yer mam. Mari Sleeth. Do ye know where she might be?"

Aoife shook her head.

"Not hiding is she?" The old woman raised her thin eyebrows and cocked her head to look around Aoife.

"No," said Aoife. "She's not home. I told you that."

The woman smiled, and a gold tooth glinted in her mouth. "That ye did."

"I can take a message for her."

The woman leaned towards Aoife and squinted. "You're the daughter, all right. It's good yer mam has you, little one. She deserves that much."

"I'm not the only daughter," Aoife snapped. Her voice surprised her.

"Aren't you, then?" The woman stared hard at Aoife. Her large, unblinking eyes made the girl flinch, and all the snap went out of Aoife in an instant. She looked down at the broom bristles.

"I'm the only daughter now." The words caught in Aoife's throat.

"No shame in that," the woman croaked. "Not yer fault the other's drowned."

Aoife felt heat rise to her face. What right had this strange woman to speak so bluntly? They never spoke of Ellen that way, never mentioned her—

"I best be going," the woman said, lurching her hunched body around toward the door. "Give your mam the message. Tell her Ol' Janny's been calling and come to see me soon."

"Old Janny?"

"We go way back, yer mam and me. More than fifteen years." Her gold tooth flashed. "Tell her to come soon. Don't forget, child. I'll know if you do."

And with that, Old Janny hobbled out.

———

THEY ATE IN SILENCE. MOTHER HARDLY LOOKED AT Aoife, and Aoife wasn't sure if she was glad for it or not. Father sipped his beer and stared at the edge of the table. Aoife was the only one who seemed to have anything waiting on her lips, but her courage had deserted her as soon as they sat down to eat. The leek soup tasted thin and bland in her mouth.

Mother sighed and pushed her chair out, getting up to clear the table.

"I—" Aoife began, but her mother's tired face stopped her.

"Something to say, love?" her father said, his voice flat. He didn't look at her.

Aoife swallowed hard. "There was a visitor today."

"A visitor?" her mother said. Not a hint of curiosity, just the words. Her mother picked up the bowls and carried them to the sink.

"Yes, an old woman." Aoife thought of Old Janny and the

hint of a threat behind her parting words. "Called herself Old Janny and asked after you, Mother."

The bowls crashed into the sink. Mother coughed and tried to make it look as if she'd meant to drop them. She took to scrubbing them furiously.

"Who now?" Father asked, his eyebrows drawing together in confusion.

"No one," Mother said quickly. "A beggar woman, I'm sure. They come after me sometimes when I'm out to market, looking for coin."

"Didn't know you were so generous," Father said.

"She said you've known each other for fifteen years," said Aoife, not letting her mother off the hook.

"And were her cheeks flushed too?" demanded Mother. "A drunkard telling tales, that's all." She scrubbed harder.

"She said to come see her soon."

"I'll do no such thing."

"But she said—"

"Aoife, enough." Her mother's voice was sharp and final.

Father slid his chair back and went to find his pipe on the wooden shelf across the room, leaving Aoife to sit alone at the rough-hewn table. The thick blue tablecloth was laid bare in front of her and the sounds of her mother's scrubbing were the only noises to be heard. Aoife sat adrift at the table, an anger welling inside, and guilt too, for she wanted to argue with her mother, but she couldn't. Not now. Not ever again. She was the only daughter. She had no right to press a knife into her mother's heart again.

No shame in that. Old Janny's words haunted her as she

lay in her cold bed that night. *Not yer fault the other's drowned.*

Her legs were getting too long for her burlap blanket, and her toes peeked out into the frosty October air. Aoife stared at her scarred feet. She could barely see the gray spots in the dark, but she knew they were there. They were ugly feet and ugly scars. No mermaid scales. Just dingy, crusted marks from the pox. Aoife squeezed her eyes shut and cursed herself for ever thinking otherwise.

Tomorrow, she'd go to the docks and find work. Maybe she could start mending nets or offer to wash the dishes at the *Busted Cork* for pennies a day. She'd pull her weight. No more pretending she wasn't what she was. No more daughter of the sea.

She had been all set to go to the docks the next morning, but when her mother had silently put on her shawl and slipped out the front door just before dawn, Aoife changed her plans and followed after. Her mother headed toward a cramped and crooked street wedged into the south part of the village. A dingy street, filled with tilted shacks and weather-worn tents, it was the poorest part of town. Aoife's family was not well-off, not by any means, but even her mother would balk at coming to this hopeless slum without good reason.

The reason hung above the doorway of a squat hut. A wooden sign, flaking with old paint, marked with the sign of two huge, round eyes.

Old Janny.

Aoife's mother went in.

Aoife herself wanted to go in too, but how could she? She waited several yards away, half hidden by a string of rags hanging out to dry in the cool early morning air. The dull rags of brown and gray flapped lightly in the breeze, and Aoife moved this way and that to stay behind their cover, out of sight. She somehow felt that Old Janny, with her owlish eyes, could see through the walls of her hut and spy intruders. But Aoife's curiosity was growing stronger than her apprehension, and when there was no sign of anyone else in that crooked street, she slipped through the folds of hanging laundry and approached the hut.

There were no windows, and the thatched straw door was shut. But the hut was rickety, built of uneven bits of tin and pine, all stuck together with odd-shaped nails, and there were a few small gaps in the walls, slits just big enough for a small eye to peek through. Aoife circled round the back of the hut and found a peephole just eye-level. She could hardly see inside, for the one-room hut was dark and lit only by candles, and some kind of spiced smoke burned from a brazier in the center of the circular room. The scent of the smoke gave off faint traces of cloves, but it reminded Aoife of stale water that had sat out for too many days.

Her mother was inside, and so was Old Janny, and they sat near each other around the brazier, but Aoife couldn't see much else and swore under her breath that she was stuck outside. She hadn't put on a coat or a shawl, and the breeze was starting to pick up. The sky was heavy with gray clouds that hung low and looked ready to burst.

Aoife put her ear to the slit in the wall and listened, plugging her other ear to keep the wind out. Old Janny started to speak, but Aoife's mother cut her off.

"You had no right to come to my house," Mother said, quick to anger.

"Don't think I haven't seen you walking sea-way, Mari," Old Janny answered. She wasn't put off by Mother's tone. There was a prying quality to Old Janny's manner, a fingernail digging out dirt from a windowsill.

"And speaking to my daughter." Aoife's mother ignored Old Janny's mention of the sea.

"Aye, your only daughter now. 'Tis a blessing you had two, now that one is gone down to the depths."

"Never mention my children again. And never bother us with your prying. What business is it of yours if I go to the seashore?"

"No business. Certainly no business." The way Old Janny said it reminded Aoife of the fishmongers in the market, always trying to entice a customer. "You may wander that way if you wish."

There was silence, and it lasted a long time. Aoife peeked her eye in again to see if her mother had left.

The two women stood facing each other, smoke slithering around them in long, winding streams.

At last, Aoife's mother said in a low voice, "Can you reverse it?"

Aoife watched as Old Janny grinned, her sunken cheeks stretching like a vulture spreading its wings.

"Reverse it?" Old Janny reached into the folds of her threadbare robe. She pulled out a heavy pouch that jangled with coins. "Can ye pay the price, Mari?"

At first, Mother's head hung down. Aoife knew what she must be thinking. What money did they have?

But then her mother nodded and said, "I'll pay it. If you promise me it will work."

"Can't make such a promise. The sea is its own master."

"Don't tell me about the sea," Aoife's mother snapped. "I'm well-acquainted with her."

"That you are," Old Janny said with a curl of her lip. "That you are."

"What's the price?"

Old Janny cocked a thin, gray eyebrow. "Same as before. Always the same."

Aoife's mother sighed and lifted her wrist, turning it so that the veins faced upward.

Old Janny untied the heavy pouch and reached inside. Aoife expected a coin, but instead, the old woman pulled out a barbed fishing hook.

Aoife's mother turned away, squeezing her eyes shut. With one swift motion, Old Janny scratched the hook across Mother's upturned wrist, tearing apart the thin flesh. Blood sprayed out, and Old Janny caught it with a small copper bowl. Then she handed Mother a frayed brown rag and waited for her to staunch the bleeding.

"Now I've paid," said Aoife's mother. "Give me my due."

"You talk as if I've crossed you. I never did nothing but give you what you asked for. Only what you asked for, Mari. I never held back."

"You said they'd inherit my blood, you said—"

"I said 'tis likely they'd inherit it. Never promised. Old Janny never promised."

"But why didn't they? Why scoop my blood into your bowl if there's no power left?"

Old Janny grinned. "There is. I can smell it." She lifted the copper bowl to her round nose and breathed in the scent of the blood.

"Give me my due." Mother's jaw was set and her chin jutted out, and Aoife couldn't help but recognize the expression that once had come so easily to her own face.

"I knew you'd come to me, Mari. I knew you'd try your luck. But whether the sea listens or no, don't return to me with regrets. I make no promises for good or for ill."

"Give me what I've paid for."

Old Janny shuffled to a dark corner of the hut, and Aoife couldn't see what she reached for. When she turned around, she carried something wrapped in a thick piece of burlap.

"You know the steps, aye? But salt water this time, Mari. Salt water, not fresh."

Aoife watched her mother take the small bundle from Old Janny, but before she turned to leave, she faced the old woman again. Even through the darkness and the smoke, Aoife could see the defiance in her mother's eyes.

"What good is my blood? What power does it have?"

Old Janny's golden teeth gleamed in the candlelight, her eyes like two lanterns. "How can ye ask me that? You of all women should know the power of the sea."

Old Janny sat by the smoking brazier, holding the bronze bowl in her lap, victory in her smile.

The wind flapped against the rags on the clothesline, startling Aoife. Pelts of hard rain were falling now, biting against her skin. She wiped water from her eyes and look again through the slit.

Her mother was gone.

The storm rolled in, clouds as dark as tar overhead. Aoife had to hurry. Already the waves might be too high.

When she got to the beach, the burlap cloth lay in the sand, sodden with rainwater. Her mother stood at the shoreline, a clam shell in her hand.

"Go back, Aoife!" she called without turning around.

The wind and the waves were so loud, Aoife knew her mother couldn't have heard her coming. And yet she knew.

"Stoke the fire and sweep the floors! This is no place for you!"

"Mother, wait!"

But her mother didn't wait. She waded into the choppy waters, the shell gripped tightly in her palm. When she was waist deep and the waves were spraying foam into her face, Aoife's mother reached down with the clam shell and scooped up a draught of water. Then she lifted the shell to her lips and drank.

Aoife expected her mother to gag on the saltiness, but what she didn't expect was for her mother to convulse and shake all over, writhing like a struck snake. And when her mother sloughed off her clothes in one violent motion, the skin beneath wasn't pinkish human flesh, but iridescent scales that glimmered in the rain. Scales and webbed hands.

Her mother dove into the water. Disappeared into the depths. The clam shell was tossed atop the waves like a lost dinghy.

Aoife didn't know what to do, but she crashed into the water anyway. Before any thought came, she grabbed the shell and scooped up a draught of sea water. She drank it, and the salt was like fire in her throat. It made every inch of her flesh shake. The waves were rising, jostling her to and fro, but she stood her ground as the water swelled over her waist. She waited for something to happen, for whatever spell Old Janny had put into the shell to work on her just as it had worked on her mother.

But nothing happened except her stomach felt sour and her throat still burned.

Then a voice from another storm sang into her head. A voice she had listened to once before.

Stop moving. Stop fighting. Just sink.

Her body felt as heavy as one of her mother's cast iron pots. There was no spell to rescue her, no transformation to take place. Just grief as powerful as an anchor.

Aoife gave in to the voice and let her body sink. She wanted her mother, and somehow her mother was down in the depths of the sea.

She sank beneath the surface, cold water covering her head, while her red hair floated all around her like willowy strands on a dorsal fin. Her body was a stone, dropping down and down into water with accelerating speed. She kept her eyes open, but the water was murky, and soon even the dim light from the stormy sky was gone, and she was surrounded by darkness.

A voice spoke out of that darkness.

"I'm back, Mother."

It was her own mother's voice. She was speaking to someone, but who it was, Aoife couldn't tell. And Aoife couldn't explain why her mother's voice sounded so clear under the water, or why neither of them had yet drowned.

They were fathoms deep. But all around her the water squeezed like a vice, and everything was black as night.

No human voice spoke in reply to Aoife's mother, but there was a sound, a long whining sound that reminded Aoife of a creaking staircase, but more melodic somehow, and melancholy. She strained to hear it, to see if some sense came from it.

"You had no right, Mother," Aoife's mother continued. "No right to take her from me."

What right had you to leave?

It was the creaking moan. Aoife could understand it now, though the sound had never changed. It felt almost like the thoughts in her head were speaking through that moan. It sounded like the voice that had told her to sink.

"I wasn't meant for the sea," replied Aoife's mother. "The surface called to me, so I went."

And left me behind. All these years.

"That's not what I wanted. I never meant to hurt you. But we're different, you and I."

Not so different. We both want back what we've lost.

"Will you return her? To dry land?"

I will keep her safe.

"No, that's not good enough for me." Aoife's mother had steel in her voice. "I've reversed the spell. You can have me again. See my scales and fins? I've given up. Keep me in your depths now. Only let my child have her chance. Let her break the surface and breathe again."

Why must she go? Why must any of you? You are daughters of the sea. Just look.

Aoife felt a swirl of bubbles cyclone around her, tickling her skin. She waved her arms and legs at the sensation.

She has your blood. They both do.

"What?" Her mother's voice drew nearer. "Oh, Aoife!"

Aoife felt cold, scaly arms wrap themselves around her, and two blue-gray eyes glinted in front of her. She couldn't see much more than the eyes, but she knew them.

"I told you to go home!" Her mother's eyes were flecked with fear, not fury. "Why must you be so stubborn!"

She turned away but kept hold of Aoife's hand. Aoife could feel the webbed flesh between her mother's fingers and the slimy scales on her hand. It reminded her of all the times she had to clean the fish her father had brought home in his nets.

"I'll stay," Aoife's mother said to the sea. "Only let my daughters go."

Aoife wanted to speak, to stop her mother from making this bargain. But would her voice even make a sound? What could she say to either her mother or the sea? Aoife felt small in that vast darkness.

You mustn't stay in these waters. You must go far away.

"I'll do it."

And you mustn't ever go to the surface again.

"I swear it."

You are a child of the sea, and the sea is where you'll stay.

"I'll pay any price."

Aoife couldn't bear it any longer. She opened her mouth to speak and felt the water rush in. But instead of drowning, she breathed the water. The salt didn't sting her throat anymore. And when it filled her lungs, it made her feel like she'd just gulped the freshest air. She found her voice.

"Mother, you can't do this!" she cried. "You can't leave us!"

Her eyes adjusted to the darkness now, and she could see the outlines of rocks and strange fish all around her. And her mother's body, the fullness of its transformation. She still had a human shape, but instead of skin, she had oily scales that shifted in color from black to green to purple, and her feet were like two fins and her hands were webbed. Her hair was gone—that auburn hair so much like Aoife's—and her face was flattened and smooth, no more contour of nose or cheek or chin. The only thing that looked like the mother Aoife had known were her eyes, still blue and human and sad.

"I'm giving you Ellen," her mother answered. "To brighten your father's heart and mend it. And you will have a sister again."

Here is the child, said the sea.

Something long and shale gray floated out from the distance, slowly coming into view as it drifted toward them. It looked like a piece of shipwreck, covered in barnacles, but it had a shape and contour that was unmistakably human. As the figure drifted by, Aoife's mother reached out her webbed hand and brushed against it. It was a tender stroke, but Aoife watched her mother's eyes flash angrily as she saw what her daughter had become.

"You said she was safe!" her mother screamed. "You said she had my blood!"

And so she does. Your blood is the only thing keeping her alive. What happens to her on dry land is no concern of mine.

"I'm going up." Aoife's mother reached out and took Ellen into her scaly arms. The girl's eyes were closed, and her barnacled form looked to Aoife like a wooden maiden carved into the prow of a ship.

That was not what you promised.

"Nor is this part of our bargain," their mother said, holding Ellen's sleeping body close to her. "I said it once before, and I'll say it again. You have no claim on me. I'll go where I will and you cannot stop me."

The sea is its own master.

Currents began to flow on either side of them. Then the currents bent toward each other, and like two snakes eating their tails, they formed a ring around them. Aoife could feel herself getting sucked down by the force of the whirlpool, and her mother too was struggling against it. Somehow she managed to grab Aoife's hand, and though no words passed between them, they knew what they must do. With every last ounce of her strength, Aoife kicked her legs and willed her body to float toward the surface. She fought against the current, against the pressure of the depths, against the cold, murky waters of this dark world, and her mother did too, and whether it was their defiance or their stubbornness that saved them, it was enough to break them free of the whirlpool's grasp.

Up and up they swam, shooting through the water like two seals, until they broke the surface, and the storm's wind slapped their faces.

"Take her!" their mother cried, thrusting Ellen's sleeping body into Aoife's arms. "Don't look back!"

Aoife barely had time to slip her arms under Ellen's and

hold her fast when their mother slipped down into the water again, disappearing as quick as a sinking rock.

The storm was still banging about, and the waves crested over Aoife's head and came crashing down on her. If she wasn't careful, the undertow would make their struggle all for naught. Her legs weak, and her chest stinging from exertion, she tried to swim to shore, but Ellen's limp body was all dead weight. Aoife struggled, but huge gulps of seawater flooded into her mouth, and this time, the water did not taste like air. It burned harsher than before, and she choked and sputtered and felt herself losing the battle.

Then her feet felt a slimy pressure against them, and a push, like hands vaulting her over a wall, and a gentler wave came at just the same time, wafting her up and toward the shore. The momentum carried her forward, her legs finding renewed strength.

She and Ellen tumbled into the wet beach, foamy waves washing all around them. Aoife dragged her sister away from the tide, up the beachhead, and it was then that she saw the clam shell, buried under an entanglement of seaweed. Her fingers reached down into the slimy muck and pulled the shell free, the grit of the wet sand clinging to its pinkish surface. She wiped it as clean as she could with her wet hair.

Ellen's eyes were closed, and though she still breathed, her chest only rose in shallow breaths, and her body was marked by shells and barnacles like the hull of an old ship.

Aoife held the shell upturned so that rainwater caught in its bowl. The pelts of rain were hard and scattered, but enough dribbled into the shell for one small sip. She held it to her sister's mouth, and with a shaking hand, she pried open

Ellen's shell-encrusted lips. It was like breaking open the thin shell of a crab's underbelly. She tilted the water into Ellen's mouth until every last drop was gone, then she gathered more from the rain. The freshest, purest water she could find, she gave to her sister, making sure that her own tears didn't mix in the bowl.

The spell had worked for Mother. It had even worked in some way for her. Now let it work for Ellen.

Aoife waited. It was the hardest waiting of all, the waiting for a life to be born. And as she waited, she couldn't help but look to the sea, toward the horizon, hoping her mother would be there, coming to join them. But the waves rose and fell and swelled with the storm, and still, her mother was nowhere in sight.

Ellen's mouth sucked in a breath as sharp as the wind. Her eyes fought against the crust of barnacles and tore themselves open. She gasped for air, her chest heaving.

Aoife cried out, joy and relief making tears spring to her eyes. She sobbed, and the tears fell all over Ellen, an endless sea of tears. Ellen started to sit up, and the two sisters found that now the barnacles flaked off her skin like dried sand. Together, they wiped away every last trace of the sea, but when she could stand again, Ellen's eyes drifted toward the water.

"I thought I heard Mother's voice..."

Aoife didn't know what to say, so she said the truth. "Our Mother is a daughter of the sea."

Ellen didn't answer. She took hold of Aoife's hand, and they both watched as the storm passed overhead and the pale sun crept out from behind distant clouds. Flecks of sunlight sparkled against the calming water. Aoife felt Ellen's hand squeeze her own, and she knew why.

Far off, almost as close to the horizon as their eyes could see, a dark figure bobbed above the water. Just for an instant, nothing more, they saw the figure raise a webbed hand.

Then it was gone.

"Come," said Aoife, her tears still kissing her cheeks. Hand in hand, she and her sister walked up the beach, back to dry land.

"Do you think, perhaps..." Ellen began as their feet hit the cobblestones of the village street.

"I don't know," Aoife answered. She knew the question Ellen was going to ask because it was her question too. "But we still have this."

Holding up her other hand, she showed Ellen the clam shell nestled in the curve of her palm.

"The rain..." Ellen's memory came back slowly. "I drank from it and..."

"Yes. Fresh this time." Aoife grinned. "But salt the next."

THE ELEMENTAL LORDS

The acolytes in the Physikos talked of nothing but the stranger known as Merlin. Phoedius was sick of hearing it. He kept his head down and buried himself in furious study whenever the conversation shifted to Merlin.

"His accent is northern. I believe he comes from the wilds beyond Gallica."

"Aeld said he saw Merlin transport into another dimension. Remember what Master Elykis said about the Eternal Plains and the immortals who live there?"

"He's no immortal. He's a man."

"He's crude, that's what he is. No culture whatsoever."

They sounded to Phoedius like a flock of noisy cranes. This Merlin was nothing more than a nuisance; why did they obsess over him?

And yet, Merlin was unavoidable. He hung around the towers and vaults of the Physikos practically day and night. Since he was not officially a member of the order, he was barred from entry, but that didn't stop Merlin from trying every trick imaginable to get in. Several weak, sickeningly insecure acolytes fed him information in the empty alleyways next to the Physikos palazzo. Some even secreted out scrolls and other texts for Merlin to study.

Phoedius was scandalized. But he made his peace with it. If he raised a fuss or told one of the masters, he would face social exclusion from the brotherhood of acolytes. Phoedius might have been misanthrope, but he was no fool. He knew he needed to maintain social connections with the other acolytes if he hoped to advance through the ranks of the order. Some day, most of these acolytes—and he himself— would be masters, and they would need to use each other for political position and power. It was always that way in the Physikos: the young needed to band together, while the old tried to keep hold of all their power.

It shouldn't have to be so, Phoedius thought. *We should be in this for the pursuit of knowledge, for the joy of discovery. Egos and other such frivolous power games should be beneath us.*

And yet, alas, they were not.

Phoedius told himself these lofty ideals, but deep down, he knew he had ambitions too. And if he should have such ambitions—he, who was more purely inspired to the noble pursuits of study and invention than his peers—then why should not the others? Such was the flaw of men. Power and ambition over the purity of knowledge and science.

Merlin, most of all, seemed nothing if not ambitious. He was not even a citizen of the empire, and yet he wanted to ingratiate himself into the very heart of its power. Phoedius suspected the strange man was up to more than studying a few contraband scrolls.

———

THE SUN HAD BARELY RISEN OVER THE OUTER HILLS OF the city when Phoedius made his way to the steel doors of the Physikos. It was so early, in fact, that the doors had not yet been unlocked. Phoedius always arrived this early—he considered it a courtesy to the masters to be punctual for his practicums—but what he did not expect was to find a disheveled figure slouched on the ground next to the entrance. A tuft of curly dark brown hair peaked out from underneath a blue hooded cloak. Snores rumbled from the man who lay under the cloak. Resting on the wall next to him was a finely crafted walking staff made of oak wood.

Phoedius knew at once that this had to be Merlin. No one else would be skulking—or sleeping—around the Physikos this early.

"Did you spend the entire night here?" Phoedius said, tapping Merlin's leg with his sandaled foot. "Or do you have an actual place you call home?"

The blue-cloaked man grunted.

Phoedius rolled his eyes and went to stand on the other side of the steel doors. He looked over to the eastern part of the city where the domes of the Lawgivers and spiraled towers of the Poets gleamed with the rosy color of dawn. Phoedius admired the artistry of the Poets' towers. The roofs of the turrets were carved to look like beds of sea coral; several of the walls were embossed with the faces and symbols of the Four Spirits: Love, Hate, Sorrow, and Joy. The carvings were meant to remind the Poets of the city that they were tasked with giving voice to the greatest desires and fears of humanity. They were the tellers of all tales. They could only compose songs and verses that spoke of the highest things, the deepest passions. Their calling was not to the mundane or the frivolous, but to the extraordinary. It was a grave responsibility, but the citizens of the Empire demanded greatness in all things.

They demanded it from the masters and the acolytes of the Physikos as well. The members of the Physikos were tasked with studying the very fabric and reality of nature itself. Nothing but total knowledge was acceptable. This suited Phoedius just fine, for he wanted nothing less than to understand the physical world in its entirety. More than that, he wanted mastery over it. He looked out at the towers of the Poets and wondered what it would be like to not only sculpt rock to look like the coral of the sea, but to command the very coral itself.

"Is that the sun?" said a groggy voice, shaking Phoedius out of his revelry. "Looks pinker than a baboon's arse."

Phoedius turned to see Merlin's head emerging from his blue hood. The mage's face was still pinched from sleep, and his eyes were glassy. In his rumpled state, Merlin looked like a scrawny street urchin, barely more than two decades old. Phoedius wondered exactly how old Merlin was. The stories that were told about the man made him seem far more experienced and world-wise than the skinny-faced youth who yawned and scratched his neck like an alley cat and half-opened his eyes to look at the locked doors of the Physikos.

"I see I came early enough," Merlin said, using his staff to push himself to his feet. "Thought I might find you here."

"Me?" Phoedius couldn't hide his surprise. "Why do you bother with me?"

"I've eavesdropped on enough conversations around this place to know that you are precisely the acolyte I need."

Phoedius scowled and waved his hand at Merlin as if he were dismissing a fly. "You've wasted your night's sleep, then. I know all about your attempts to enter the Physikos—the way you've tried to bribe my peers, the way you've convinced weaker men to sneak valuable scrolls out here so you can violate the laws of our order. I tell you now, directly, without hesitation, that you shall never get any help in that regard from me. I would rather give up my studies and aspirations to be a master than give out one ounce of assistance to you."

Merlin brushed a tangle of curly dark hair out of his eyes. "I see. Very well." He shrugged. "I suppose I'll withdraw my offer then. I thought for sure you would want to walk along the bottom of the ocean with me, but I can see I was mistaken. You're not the man I'm looking for after all."

Merlin turned and abruptly started to walk from the palazzo of the Physikos to a narrow street that jutted off to the west.

Phoedius couldn't quite comprehend what he'd just heard. Had Merlin mentioned walking along the seafloor? It was absurd. A jest. Phoedius turned back to the steel doors and waited for the porters to come and open them. He tried to put Merlin out of his mind.

But Merlin would not leave his thoughts.

What had the stranger possibly meant? Had he acquired an underwater vessel?

But Phoedius knew that was unlikely; the masters who made such vehicles would never let an outsider like Merlin use them. And didn't Merlin say "walk"? Had Merlin devised a contraption that would let them walk underwater without drowning?

Phoedius was overcome with curiosity. The sun had found its resting place in the early morning sky, and the porters would be along any minute to open the doors to the Physikos. But Phoedius would not be there to watch them. For the first time in five years—since becoming an acolyte and gaining entrance to the great Physikos of Atlantis—Phoedius would not be going to his laboratory. He would not be starting his day's work. He would not be preparing Master Elykis's classroom for the practicum, or organizing the scrolls for mid-morning study.

Instead, Phoedius turned from the Physikos and followed after Merlin. He dogged the mage's steps for several blocks, keeping silent and trying to escape Merlin's notice. But as they traveled deeper and deeper into the city's slums, Phoedius finally made himself known.

"Are you trying to drive me off?" He tugged on Merlin's blue cloak and spoke in a whisper. "This is no place for decent citizens."

Merlin stopped but did not turn around to face his follower. "If you can believe it, I had no idea you were behind me."

"I don't believe it," replied Phoedius. "You wanted me to follow you."

"Nevertheless, I didn't think you would. Your rejection of my offer was pretty definitive. Wouldn't give me an 'ounce of assistance' you said. Your words, not mine. So I took you at your word."

Phoedius scoffed. "Do you dare pretend that you are honest and straightforward? I know what you are, Merlin. Do not play innocent with me."

Merlin turned around to face the acolyte. He was smiling. "It's only a little further. I'll protect you from the unsavory characters."

Then he started walking again, turning down a narrow street that was little more than a crevice between two dilapidated buildings made of stone. Stone meant this was the oldest part of the city, before the masters of the Physikos had figured out how to craft steel and build the wonders of the outer hills—the domes and spires that illuminated Atlantis' glory. Phoedius could see that barely anyone inhabited this crumbling stone neighborhood now.

He almost turned back. He considered retracing his steps to the Physikos and putting all this Merlin business behind him. Nothing good would come of following Merlin through this deserted ruin. For a brief moment, he worried that Merlin was going to rob him or commit some act of violence against him. There was no one around to witness anything. A perfect place for a crime.

But instead of acquiescing to his fears, Phoedius followed Merlin down the narrow alleyway.

Merlin stopped in front of a rotting wooden door. No one had bothered to put a lock on such a door.

"I thought you promised to take me walking along the ocean floor," Phoedius said.

"In due time," replied Merlin. Gingerly, he pushed the door open and motioned Phoedius inside. "After you."

The door led to a darkened, cave-like room. Phoedius had never seen a more cluttered or grimy place. The floor was dirty, the smell dank and musky. In the far corner was a cot covered in matted straw that looked unsuitable even for pigs.

"You live here?" Phoedius couldn't mask the disgust in his voice.

"Well, we can't all live in the acolytes' apartments."

"You are no acolyte."

"Hence this room."

Phoedius tried not to gag, but the room smelled strongly of wet fur and rotting fish.

"Right," Merlin replied, seeing the disgust on the acolyte's face. "That would be Bedwyn. He was probably out fishing last night."

"Bedwyn? You have a companion with you?"

"I need someone to talk to."

"Is he one of your own people? From the north?"

Merlin grinned. "I would not say that."

Phoedius almost screamed. From out of the darkness, behind a pile of scrap metals, two rows of gleaming white fangs snarled at him.

"It's alright, Bedwyn," Merlin said calmly. "I invited him."

The fangs disappeared behind lips and a long snout. Phoedius heard a low grunt come from the snout.

Merlin spoke a muffled word under his breath and two lamps illuminated on a crooked table nearby.

This time Phoedius did indeed yelp. It was a kind of a hiccuping yelp that caught the acolyte off-guard. He was embarrassed to discover that his hands were shaking, but he couldn't quite believe what he was seeing.

The fangs and snout which had snarled at him belonged to a gray-haired baboon. It sat on its haunches and eyed the acolyte with beady, unblinking eyes.

"W-w-what?" began Phoedius.

"Introductions are in order, I think," said Merlin. "Go on, Bedwyn. Don't be rude."

The baboon snorted and scratched under its arm for a bug. It found one, chewed on it for a bit, then spit it out at Phoedius.

"Be nice," Merlin continued. "This man is here to help us."

Bedwyn looked at Merlin, and Phoedius was sure the primate gave the mage an almost human look of exasperation. Then the baboon started circling around Phoedius, sniffing his robes and sandals. It took a finger and twirled it around Phoedius's long gray hair.

"Merlin," said Phoedius, "I must insist that you make this beast stand down."

"I have a name, you know."

Phoedius's heart nearly stopped. The baboon had spoken. Human words. In the tongue of the Atlanteans.

"Settle down, Bedwyn," Merlin said. "Phoedius has had a long morning. Give him some room, will you?"

The baboon shrugged—letting go of Phoedius's hair—and moved over to the crooked table to sit down.

"He speaks," Phoedius hissed. "He speaks. Like a human. He speaks."

"Yes, you've certainly made a striking discovery," the baboon replied. "I do speak. Well done." The baboon turned to the mage, "I say, Merlin, is this really the one you were waiting for? He seems a bit thick if you ask me."

"But how?" Phoedius was still in shock. "There are masters who have worked for decades to communicate with the animal kingdom, and only minimal progress has been made."

"Have they really?" Merlin asked, eyes brightening. "That's just the sort of thing I was hoping to learn from you. What the masters have been doing. What goes on inside that giant steel school of yours. Tell me," Merlin said, grinning, "what methods have the masters tried?"

"But..." Phoedius struggled to put words to his lips. "Why should you want to know? You've already mastered the art yourself."

"That shouldn't matter. What matters is the pursuit of knowledge. Knowledge about the world and its workings. Isn't that why we're both here? Isn't that why you are an acolyte of the Physikos and I am a sneak who's been trying to get in? Perhaps my way of doing things isn't the only way. Perhaps it is. But how can I ever know unless I seek out that knowledge? The vastness of what human beings are capable of is inexhaustible. Satisfy my curiosity. Feed my hunger."

Phoedius knew exactly the hunger Merlin was talking about. He had felt it too, gnawing at him, driving him to leave his mother and his old friends behind, coaxing him to enter the order of acolytes. The hunger for knowledge spurred him to study five different disciplines when most of his peers only studied three; the insatiable desires of his curiosity made him nearly friendless since all of his time—all of his pursuits—were directed toward study and work and research. Phoedius wanted to reach the utter limits of what a person could know. He began to wonder if Merlin might help him do it.

While he wondered all this, Phoedius stood mute before Merlin's expectant face.

"You've brought home a dull one," Bedwyn grumbled. "Throw him back through the door."

"Give him time," Merlin reassured the baboon. "It's still early. Go on, Phoedius, tell me about the masters' experiments."

Phoedius knew he should not share the secrets of the Physikos with this stranger. But his mouth opened anyway and the secrets spilled out. "Telepathy. Psychic connections. Some of the bolder masters experimented with surgeries and other procedures meant to alter the animals' brains, but those experiments have been failures so far."

"Surgeries?" Merlin frowned.

"Butchery!" exclaimed the baboon. "Foul, ignoble butchery!"

Merlin put a hand on the baboon's back. "I agree," Merlin said, his voice now flat and low. "How disappointing. Just goes to show."

Phoedius wanted to inquire into what Merlin meant, but the young mage was suddenly rummaging through a brass chest on the floor.

"Aha!" he said, seizing upon something inside the chest. His hand emerged holding a conch shell. "Ready for our walk?"

"Will you tell me how you made that baboon talk?"

Merlin laughed. "In due time. But right now I'm ready for my morning bath."

———

A DENSE FOG HAD SETTLED OVER THE WESTERN HARBOR. Dozens of gigantic crabs and dolphins and eels floated placidly in the docks. Their metallic bodies occasionally clanged against the wood of the piers, making a dull sort of music in the early morning. It was the only sound to be heard—except for the lapping of the gentle waves. The fog was too thick for sailing or fishing, so most seafarers were not out yet. Their ships were left to float restlessly in the piers.

Merlin stood at the edge of one of the long barnacled docks and peered out into the thick soup of mist. Phoedius stood nearby, but his eyes darted all around, keeping a lookout for anyone from the Physikos who might recognize him. The last thing the acolyte wanted was to be spotted hanging around with Merlin.

"I thought the fleet was off charting new waters or conquering some other kingdom," said Merlin, pointing to the ships anchored in the harbor.

Phoedius scoffed. "These few ships are not the fleet," he said, motioning to the steel ships. "They are fishing vessels and patrol ships."

"They're ingenious. And a bit fanciful, I have to admit. I particularly like the purple eel with the three eyes."

"Those are portholes, not eyes."

"Yes, but they're made to look like eyes. Crafted by the welders?"

"Indeed," said Phoedius. "But designed by the masters of the Physikos."

"Of course," Merlin said grinning at the acolyte. "Which is exactly why I want to know more about the work you do there. All the secrets and best laid plans."

"What is the conch shell for, if I may ask?" Phoedius said, changing the subject.

"For asking permission. My powers aren't what you guess them to be. I don't command nature. Quite the opposite, in fact."

Merlin raised the conch shell to his lips and began whispering to it. Phoedius strained to hear what Merlin said, but the mage's words were indecipherable. It didn't matter anyway. Something infinitely more interesting was happening to the sea.

The water began to bubble. It was like a fire had been lit under the sea and now the harbor was boiling. Then the water started churning and waves started crashing. The ships that were docked in the harbor began to sway and beat against the piers. Phoedius watched in astonishment as the water along the edge of the docks started receding, as if some kind of drain several hundred feet out from shore had been opened and the sea water was being sucked down it. The fog, too, was sucked away by whatever force was draining the harbor. Sand and seaweed and crustaceans were exposed to the open air. The water kept receding, forming a pathway that led out from the dock into the wider sea.

Merlin took the conch shell, hopped down from the dock, and scooped up what little water remained in puddles along the harbor. Then he drank from the shell.

"Better take a swig," he said, handing it up to Phoedius.

Phoedius took the shell, unthinking, and sipped from the salty water inside. He coughed and gagged—but then as soon as his throat started to tighten, it loosened again, and the bitter saltiness disappeared. It tasted like clear fresh water.

Merlin nodded and took the shell back from Phoedius. "Ready?"

Merlin started to walk out into the sea. Phoedius teetered on the edge of the dock. His feet hesitated. His heart did not.

Sandaled feet sank into wet sand.

Merlin spoke strange words in a language Phoedius did not know. At once, the sea flooded over them. Phoedius smiled as he realized that he was breathing underwater. He followed Merlin into the deep—into the midnight of the ocean, where no Atlantean had ever traveled before.

———

"MASTER ELYKIS?" PHOEDIUS STOOD IN THE HALLWAY outside the master's private chamber.

Elykis was snoring in his chair. The man was so old that his skin had begun to turn a dark gray. His hair sprouted out of his head in haphazard tufts, like the feathery white florets of a dandelion. With each snore, the sagging skin under his neck wriggled and his thin hair waved.

"Master," Phoedius repeated, trying to make his tone a bit sharper without being too harsh. "Master, please wake."

The old master stirred, half-opened his eyes, then went back to snoring.

Phoedius inched into the room. He wished Elykis would wake up, but there was also a part of himself that hoped the master would continue to sleep. Phoedius had come to speak with Elykis about Merlin, but now that he was here, standing in the room, listening to the phlegmatic snores of his master, he was starting to reconsider. What would Elykis say, except to stay away from Merlin? Phoedius knew the advice already; there was no need to ask.

And if the acolyte was truly honest with himself, he would admit that he did not want to stay away from Merlin. His mind drifted back to their walk at the bottom of the ocean. He laughed to himself when he thought of his reaction to those monstrous fish that glowed like lanterns in the darkest waters. Merlin had been so calm, so unperturbed by it all. In his mind's eye, Phoedius could still see Merlin's grin as he stood triumphant on the ocean floor. The mage's white teeth gleamed, his pale blue eyes crinkled with mischief. Phoedius wondered if Merlin might consent to take him exploring again.

Phoedius stopped. He was half-way to Elykis's chair, but he decided not to wake the master. Slowly, he turned to leave the chamber.

The whirl of mechanical gears and the soft grinding of steel against steel stopped Phoedius in his tracks.

"Eh?" came the sleepy, hoarse voice of Elykis. "What's this? What's this?"

Phoedius tried to compose himself, to make it seem as if he had just wandered in.

"Waking me from my slumber, eh, Pandaros?" Elykis heaved himself up from his chair, bones creaking as loudly as the gears of the creature in the corner of the room. "And on such a hot day too. You wouldn't know it, though, would you, you pile of metal?"

Phoedius turned to face his master. Not far from Elykis's chair, stuffed between two massive piles of used vellum, was a mechanical albatross, its body crafted of steel and its innards made of copper gears. It waddled out from its hiding place and clicked its beak at Phoedius.

"Oh, it's you," said Elykis, seeing Phoedius for the first time. "So you're the one who woke me up. Don't fret. I needed to get up anyway. Azaraz is coming to show me his latest design for the extra-spacial cloth we've been working on. I still say it would work best as a garment, but old Az is convinced the Imperial generals would be more impressed if we used it as a saddle bag."

Elykis began puttering around in a corner of the room, lifting scrolls and writing tablets, looking for something buried beneath them.

"Ah!" he said, holding up a wide piece of woolen fabric. The fabric was utterly nondescript, but the way Elykis handled it made it seem like the finest silk. "What do you say, Phoedius? Cloak or carrying bag?"

"Isn't the idea to make more of it?" Phoedius said as calmly as he could. "Why does it matter what you do with this sample?"

The old master smiled. His pale pink eyes gently

mocked the acolyte. "You really don't like to play politics, do you? Of course we'll make more of the cloth. But we need patronage. Need to impress those who hold the purse strings. And in my opinion, making a man disappear beneath a cloak is much more impressive than stuffing a bunch of junk in a bag."

"As you say, Master."

"Bah! You're no fun, Phoedius." The master picked up a peacock feather fan that was lying near his chair and began to fan himself. "Hot one, isn't it? Makes a person want to sleep until dusk and hope that the weather cools or a storm comes. Anyway, I know you didn't come to hear me discuss the weather. What's your business? You must have had a reason to disturb my beautiful dreams."

Phoedius was caught. He had nothing to ask the master except the question about Merlin, and now that the moment was at hand, Phoedius knew he would never say a word to Elykis about the mage. He looked quickly about the room, wracking his brain to find an excuse. His eyes settled on the albatross, which stood waiting for an answer as patiently as its master.

"Pandaros," Phoedius said, his voice steady though his heart was pounding. "I wondered if I might borrow him for some work I'm doing with weather patterns and fish populations off the western coast."

"Weather patterns? Fish?" Elykis narrowed his eyes. The fan slowed down its waving. "When did this particular avenue of scholarship pop into your head? I can't blame you, what with this heat wave we've been having. However, I was under the impression you were getting ready to help young

Aeld with his work on temporal measurements and manipulation."

Phoedius tried to stay calm, but he could feel his legs beginning to shake. "Yes, Aeld. Correct. I was going to help him." Phoedius paused for an inordinate amount of time. His mind was a total blank; he couldn't think of any explanation for this sudden change in his research plans.

Elykis waved his fan in Phoedius's direction and pretended to look stern, but Phoedius could see the twinkle in the old man's pale pink eyes. "Fine, fine. Take the old bird. He's been pestering me with his creaking gears all week. Be sure to grab a bottle of oil, or you'll develop a terrible headache from all the wheezing and grinding."

Phoedius hastened out of the master's chamber, the mechanical albatross in tow. He barely caught a glimpse of Master Elykis settling back into his chair, the peacock feather fan waving lazily.

"Remember," Elykis called, "get some oil!"

———

PHOEDIUS NEVER GOT THE OIL FOR THE ALBATROSS'S gears. His mind was consumed with other things. Merlin had gotten too strong a hold on him.

"I'm going to show you a new trick." Merlin sat on a low, crumbling wall of stone that formed an alleyway near his lodgings. He was swinging his legs like an overeager boy. The staff made of oak lay carelessly across his lap.

Phoedius wasn't quite sure how he had ended up near

Merlin's residence. He had been going to buy more vellum at one of the shops near the Poets' towers, but somehow, he ended up in the slum where Merlin lived.

"Better come inside," Merlin added. "Not that anyone usually comes strolling down this sewer. But still. Secrets of the Faerie realm should remain secrets. Don't worry; I sent Bedwyn out for some lunch."

"So it's true then? Faerie? You come from another dimension?" Phoedius tried to keep his voice calm, but his hands betrayed him. His fingers twitched with excitement.

"Truth is not something you should tempt me with, Phoedius. Least of all the truth about Faerie." Merlin eyed the quivering fingers. "You really should see if the masters have anything for that nervous tick, my friend. It will betray you."

Merlin hopped down from the derelict wall, and with quick strides, made his way inside the hovel. At times Merlin could seem so childlike, at other times so dangerous. Phoedius buried his hands in his robes and followed.

The room inside was dark. The baboon was nowhere in sight.

Merlin tapped his staff on the floor twice and three misshapen candles lighted. Flames appeared out of nowhere.

"You want to know things, don't you, Phoedius?" Merlin whispered. "Like how I made fire ignite from nothing."

"The masters would hypothesize that you used a chemical compound or some other natural means."

"I used natural means, but not in the way the masters think."

"Yes," Phoedius said, his voice now a whisper, afraid that somehow his words would be heard all the way to the Physikos. "But the masters' minds are limited. They see the world and its elements as merely tools in service to the Empire."

"And you're not interested in tools? My staff, after all, is a tool."

"You obfuscate, Merlin. It is much more than a tool."

Merlin grinned. "In such a short time, and how well you know me."

"As you said," Phoedius replied, smiling as well, "I want to know things."

Merlin came close to Phoedius—so close that the acolyte could smell the days' old sweat that clung to Merlin's cloak. Reaching up a hand, Merlin grasped a strand of Phoedius's silvery hair in his fingers. Then he plucked.

Phoedius flinched a little, but did not question Merlin. Somehow, he knew not to question him.

Merlin wrapped the strand of hair around the oaken staff. Then—speaking in words that were not like any human sound Phoedius had ever heard—Merlin spoke to the staff and pressed the strand of hair against his neck.

Merlin's skin melted away, replaced by the grayish skin tone that characterized all Atlanteans. Merlin's body stretched and thinned out. His eyes were closed, but when he opened them, they were colored pink like the sky at sunset. His face became all angles—a thin, wide mouth; a pointed chin; a nose that was slender and feminine.

Phoedius's breath caught in his throat. He was staring at

his own face, his own body, his own form—living and breathing before his eyes. Merlin had ceased to be Merlin and was instead an exact copy of Phoedius himself.

"Have they found a chemical compound for this?" said Merlin-as-Phoedius.

"Why do you want to get inside the Physikos? There is nothing inside for you to learn. Nothing." It was all Phoedius could think to say.

"Nevertheless," Merlin replied, "I want to. The question is: Are you ready? And do you have anything of Master Elykis's?"

———

PANDAROS COCKED ITS HEAD WHEN PHOEDIUS AND A hooded man shaped much like Phoedius entered the acolyte's apartment.

Merlin dropped his blue hood and the mechanical albatross saw two identical faces peering back at him.

"The bird is confused," Phoedius said.

"My magic may impress you," answered Merlin, "but I can't quite believe this fantastic creation is real." Merlin went over to the mechanical albatross and knelt down to inspect it more thoroughly. "Hello there," he said, peering at the albatross's underbelly. Pandaros snipped at Merlin's nose, but instead of being upset, the mage just laughed. "He knows something's not right."

Phoedius almost told Merlin about the psychic links the masters were able to establish between automatons and

Atlanteans. It was the same technology that powered the water vessels and made the empire's fleet the most deadly and efficient in the world. It was hard for enemies to defend against ships that could respond to the instantaneous thoughts and feelings of their captains. The same was true of Pandaros. The bird rejected Merlin-as-Phoedius because there was no link to be made with Merlin's mind.

Why Phoedius kept this information from Merlin, the acolyte couldn't say. Something within him began to pull away from Merlin, to doubt a man who could have such power as to alter reality itself. Phoedius was both overwhelmed with wonder and seized with terror at Merlin's transformation. A man who could change his appearance at will was a dangerous man.

"Ready, my friend?" Merlin said. It was unsettling to see the mage's smile curl over Phoedius's own lips. Phoedius had to remind himself that what he was seeing was not some twisted reflection, but really Merlin in disguise.

"How can I answer if you won't tell me what you have in mind?" said Phoedius.

"Put your hand on the bird and wait for a bit of fairy magic, will you?"

Phoedius did as he was told. Despite his growing unease with Merlin, he couldn't reject him. He placed a shaking hand on the smooth, cool head of the steel albatross.

Merlin touched the shaft of his oaken staff to Phoedius's hand. Then, speaking the same incomprehensible words, Merlin's eyes rolled back into his head. Phoedius felt nothing, but he watched in horror as his hand bloated and turned a dark gray. Yellowish liver spots sprouted along his skin. His arm became flabby and much shorter than it should have been.

Phoedius knew at once what had happened. Just as Merlin had transformed himself into Phoedius, Phoedius had been transformed into Master Elykis.

"Now," said Merlin, pinkish eyes twinkling with mischief, "we go to the Physikos."

———

GETTING INTO THE PHYSIKOS WAS SIMPLE. NONE OF THE door wardens questioned or even gave a second glance to Master Elykis and his acolyte as they entered through the steel doors.

Phoedius was ill at ease in his guise as Elykis, but fortunately, the real Elykis suffered from a sickness of the joints that made him walk in a halting, shuffling kind of way, and Phoedius found such a walk suited his nervous, guilty-ridden psyche.

Merlin, meanwhile, was doing his best impression of Phoedius, striding with overly-serious determination and dignity. Phoedius wondered with some embarrassment if he really did walk in such a supercilious way. As they passed by a cluster of acolytes who bowed with exaggerated respect for the man they thought was Elykis, Merlin ever-so-slightly stuck his nose in the air. Then, when they were safely past the acolytes, the mage winked and gave Phoedius a little smirk.

"The power of glamour," he said.

Phoedius felt sick.

In Elykis's private chamber, Merlin was more giddy than a child with a bag of sweets. He flitted from contraption to contraption, from scroll to scroll, every object a new delight. His fingers drifted over the bright-colored feathers of the fan on Elykis's desk. He confessed that he had never seen such feathers before, and Phoedius explained that they came from a foreign bird known as a peacock.

"And this?" Merlin said, holding up the extra-spacial woolen cloth.

Phoedius almost lied, but somehow the truth tumbled from his lips. "It bends the dimension of physical space. Cover an object or a person with it and it will seem like there is nothing there."

Merlin's eyes—which in appearance were the eyes of Phoedius—lit up with pleasure. It was a look that Phoedius had never truly seen on his own face before.

Soon Phoedius found himself explaining other items to Merlin's eager inquiries: a bronze disk fashioned to look like the face of the sun; a water-stone made from a rare form of flint that the wild tribes of Latinum called "razor rock;" a looking-glass that showed the living image of the Imperial Courtyard instead of one's own reflection. Merlin didn't just want to know the names and properties of the items, he wanted to know the theories and methods behind their creation. Phoedius could hardly keep up with Merlin's inquiries; the mage's desire to know was insatiable.

Phoedius was exhilarated. Finally, he could talk to someone else who loved the wild possibilities of science, experimentation, and creation the way he did. All the other acolytes would never have been so unabashedly eager to know and to learn the way Merlin was. For the acolytes, life in the Physikos was about making connections, apprenticing with the right people, jockeying for position within the ranks —study and inquiry and the thrill of new knowledge was hardly an afterthought. But Merlin—this stranger, this outsider—had more passion, more sincere love of the mysteries of nature, than all the acolytes and most of the masters combined.

Phoedius almost forgot that he was disguised with Master Elykis's face. He almost forgot that he had committed a crime against the Physikos by letting Merlin gain entrance to a master's private chambers. But one glance at his transformed face in a nearby mirror reminded Phoedius that he had betrayed one of the few good men he knew.

"It is my turn for questions," Phoedius said, his eyes locked with the false eyes of Master Elykis in the mirror. "How did you do this? How did you give me the face of another man?"

Merlin sighed. "It is magic, my friend. Yes, the stuff of children's tales and forgotten myths. You deal in science— wondrous, glorious, reality-bending science. But my way is an older way. And this magic—the magic called glamour—is older still. If I told you how to work such magic, the fairies would come and cut off my toes." Merlin grinned and began fiddling around with a miniature weathervane.

Phoedius shook his head. "You tease me, Merlin."

"I do not. Fairies are spiteful little creatures."

"We had better go. The master will be back soon."

Phoedius seemed to have cursed them with his words. Master Elykis's voice could be heard faintly out in the hall.

Phoedius froze. Merlin looked at the closed door with mild interest, but he continued to casually handle the weathervane as if nothing was amiss. The master's voice gradually crescendoed with every second that Merlin and Phoedius stayed in the room.

"Merlin!" Phoedius hissed.

Merlin shrugged and set the weathervane down without a second glance. "There's a window, after all. Nothing to fear."

Before Phoedius could make sense of Merlin's comment, the mage had plucked a feather from Elykis's peacock feather fan. Brushing the feather across his forehead and Phoedius's, Merlin spoke the words of transformation.

Phoedius tried to imagine the master's face upon entered his private chamber, the colorful plumes of two peacocks diving out the open window and disappearing.

———

PEACOCKS DO NOT FLY FAR OR PARTICULARLY WELL, BUT they can fly well enough to get to safety. Phoedius and Merlin landed in an empty street, and with what seemed like a snap of his fingers, Merlin had transformed them back into themselves.

Phoedius said nothing for a long while. He could hardly find words to describe the impossible sensation of flight: the mix of weightlessness and solidity in his body; the knife-like sharpness of the air against his feathers. He tried to remember everything about his flight even as it drifted away like a dream.

They walked down several streets; Phoedius was in a daze, but Merlin followed his lead. It was only after several minutes and a long, circuitous route that Phoedius looked up and realized he had led them to the Poets' towers.

Without a word, Phoedius took Merlin into the nearest tower, a gleaming salmon-colored facade that was engraved with images of the most fearsome monsters of the Old Realm. As with so much about the empire and its secrets, Merlin asked questions. Phoedius told the story of the fearsome daemon of the sea, Mearax—a six-headed giant with nine tentacled arms that devoured any man who dared sail out into the wide western ocean. Mearax had rows of teeth like a shark, and spewed salt water, drowning ships and sailors who dared disturb his seas.

"Sounds like a god," Merlin said, admiring the images of Mearax on the walls of the tower. "We have a sea god too, where I'm from."

"Mearax was no god. He was a monster. And besides, he was destroyed. The first lords of the Old Realm butchered him. They commanded the earth to rise up and crush him."

"What invention did they use? What science?"

Phoedius frowned. "They knew the elements. As you do."

Merlin said nothing.

"And then they studied his body parts to better understand how such a creature came to be, how it moved and lived and ruled the ocean."

"The beginning of the Physikos, then?"

Phoedius went over to the open stone archway that led into the tower. There were no doors on the Poets' towers, no wardens, no gates. All were free to listen to the songs and stories of the poets and to enjoy their pleasures. Phoedius had not entered such archways since he was a small boy. For a brief moment, he could hear his mother's laugh, remember her scent. She had always loved the freedom of the towers.

"No disguises this time," he told Merlin as they entered the open courtyard. The place was empty, except for a gallery of statues, each of them carved from sandstone, and each depicting some great figure from the Atlantean past.

"The lords of the Old Realm?" Merlin asked.

But Phoedius gave no answer.

In the center of the courtyard—supported only by one strong steel beam as its anchor—was a spiral staircase that made its way to the very top of the cloud-touching tower.

"No wings this time," Phoedius said. He ascended the staircase. Merlin followed wordlessly.

At the top was a small observatory, a balcony that opened to the skies over Atlantis. The imperial city spread out beyond the sight of mortal eyes, as large as a continent. The sun was beginning to set, the clouds tinged with frothy pink. Merlin's blue cloak was caught up in the wind and billowed behind him. Phoedius watched as the young mage's eyes gazed at the expanse of the city. He saw something he had never seen on Merlin's face before: frailty.

"Who are your gods," Phoedius began, "from the place where you come?"

Merlin continued to look out over the city; his face was like a stone mask. "Like all gods, I suppose. Powerful and alluring."

"We in Atlantis have no gods, save the god of conquest. A

self-made god that should lie in the heart of every true Atlantean."

"But not you."

"No, not me. My god is fire. It is water. It is earth and air. My god is knowledge. Discovery. Exploring the world for the sake of nothing more than to understand it."

Merlin smiled and looked at Phoedius. "An inexhaustible quest."

"I know." Phoedius smiled too. "But you have unlocked some of the secrets, haven't you?"

"I'm lord of the elements, is that it?"

"Like the men and women of the Old Realm." Phoedius looked to the coral-covered roofs of the other towers. "There's a lot of gossip about you, you know. Where you come from, who you are."

"I've come from a lot of places."

"Yes, but only one is the truth."

Merlin looked back out at the expanse of the city. "Do you know what this place is missing? A forest. A great, big rambling forest, crowded with trees. Oak, elm, willow."

"There are the gardens of Ilaria."

"Not the same. I'm talking about wild, uncharted forests that cover half an island and stir the hearts of even the gods themselves."

"Your home?"

Merlin nodded. "It has no name yet. It is too wild for that. Only a few of us mortal men even live there. But it has more beauty in it than all of these towers and domes and gardens put together."

"You miss it."

"Perhaps."

"Then why did you leave?"

Merlin wrapped his cloak around himself as if he were chilled by the wind. Then he turned to Phoedius again and leaned in close to whisper in the acolyte's ear.

"Same as you. Knowledge."

"Tell me about it, the woods where you come from."

Merlin spoke, and when he spoke, his voice was soft and unguarded, different from any way he had spoken with Phoedius before. He told the acolyte about the cool darkness of the forests that blanketed his island home. He spoke of the frosty songs of morning, the larks and robins, the chittering of squirrels. He sighed for the lilacs and the pines. He laughed when he told about the languages of trees, and how he had spent six days convincing an old oak to give up one of its limbs for the honor of being made into Merlin's staff. It seemed to Phoedius that as Merlin spoke, the mage almost forgot the acolyte was there. He spoke to himself, to a part of himself that he longed for and was trying to find again.

Phoedius envied Merlin this longing. He closed his eyes and tried to imagine an uncharted world untouched by the corruption of the empire.

The sun was below the horizon now, and the sky was turning the dull yellow-gray of late evening.

"We had better go," said Phoedius. "Thank you for today, Merlin. And thank you for your..." Phoedius hesitated at the word.

"Friendship?"

Phoedius realized his hands had begun to shake.

"Thank you for this," said Merlin, waving his hands at

the panorama of the city. "I've never seen Atlantis from this height. Nor have I been to a Poet's tower."

"My mother used to take me here," Phoedius began. "I haven't been back since I joined the order of the Physikos. There didn't seem a need."

There was a long silence. The two men stared out over the city.

"Never make me break the laws of the Physikos again, Merlin."

The laughing, mischievous eyes of the mage returned, the moment of frailty gone. "I promise," he said.

———

THE IMPERIAL GUARD CAME IN THE DARKEST PART OF night. They broke the handle on the door and moved swiftly. Phoedius barely had time to cover himself with a nightshirt. He had no time to put on sandals.

With rough shoves from the blunt ends of spears, Phoedius was taken from his apartment, shackled with chains, and thrown into a mold-infested dungeon below the domes of the Lawgivers.

It wasn't until the third day that they gave him any food. A latch lifted, a small hatch opened at the bottom of the door, and unseen hands slid a plate of rubbery octopus across the damp floor. Phoedius devoured the octopus even though he could taste the rancid sourness of its rotten flesh. They gave him no water, so he slurped up what dribbles he could from the puddles that covered the floor.

By the fifth day, he had almost lost his mind.

By the sixth day, he had a visitor.

"It's alright, my good fellow." The voice of Master Elykis rang out in the echoing tunnels outside Phoedius's cell. "I know this man. I'm the one he is supposed to have stolen from."

The guard let the master in.

Phoedius tried to hide in the corner shadows of his cell when the master entered. After five days in damp filth and darkness, Phoedius was ashamed. But the master, hobbling in with some difficult across the slick, wet floor, smiled pleasantly as if they were in one of the laboratories testing an alchemic formula.

"Phoedius," the master said softly, kindly. "I hope you won't mind my coming."

Phoedius shivered and exhaled slightly. His lips were too dry for talking.

"Are you alright? How have they treated you?" the master continued. "Bah! What am I saying? Of course they've been treating you like dung. This is the Imperial Guard we're talking about, isn't it? What fools. And you are a victim of their cowardice and insecurity. Calm down, my boy. I know you did not steal anything from my private chambers. You may a bit of a cold fish, but you're no thief. And why in the name of the celestial planets would you take that unimpressive temporal disk? No, no, it wasn't you. But, alas, the Council does not believe my testimony."

"Wh-wh-why am I here?" Phoedius gasped.

Elykis raised his eyebrows. "You mean you haven't been told the charges? Nothing about the crime you're supposed to have committed? I knew our government was corrupt, but I had no idea it was this incompetent! You've been accused of stealing from the Physikos. The temporal disk, the extraspacial cloth, and the water-stone from Latinum. Eyewitnesses saw you enter my chamber. Several door wardens and passersby on the street recognized you and said you were carrying a satchel full of the items from my room. It's all ridiculous, of course. Eye-witnesses can be notoriously unreliable."

"Saw me?" Phoedius managed. It was impossible. He had not been back to the Physikos since he took Merlin there. He hadn't had the courage to return; instead, he had stayed in his rooms and sulked. He hadn't heard from Merlin since that day either; no more requests to sneak into the Physikos, no more questions about the work of the masters. It was like Merlin had disappeared.

"I can't explain it, frankly," Elykis continued, "except to say that these witnesses are mistaken. I hadn't seen you in the Physikos for several days, in fact, and yet all of these citizens claimed to have seen your face."

Phoedius's hand slowly brushed his own cheek. His fingers twitched as they touched the skin. "My face."

"Yes. There must be another man in this city who shares your looks, and for that coincidence, you are now being condemned. Of course, some of the door wardens mentioned seeing that nervous twitch in your fingers as you rushed out. You do have that habit, don't you? The testimony of the wardens sealed your fate, I'm afraid How this other man would've known that, I'm not sure." Elykis shook his head.

But Phoedius knew. *You really should see if the masters have anything for that nervous tick, my friend. It will betray you.* The words formed in Phoedius's mind, as clear as the pale blue eyes of the man who had spoken them.

Elykis reached out a hand toward Phoedius's shoulder, but the imprisoned man recoiled. "Of course," Elykis said, bowing his head. "I shouldn't be so familiar. But trust me, Phoedius, I shall do what I can to convince the Council of your innocence."

Innocence. The word lingered in the air like the musty smell of the wet straw piled in the corner of the cell. Phoedius hated the word. It was a lie. He felt no innocence. He felt his own guilt like a festering wound. He knew the face that had stolen those things from Elykis. It had been his own face. Worn by a man who wielded magic. And Phoedius had shown him the way.

————

THE COUNCIL OF TWELVE WORE SILVER HOODS OVER their faces and sat on a high dais that towered twenty feet over the assembly. No one knew who sat on the Council. They wore their hoods whenever they presided over judgments, and they lived together in the private gardens of Ilaria—the designated home for the Council of Twelve. They never came out into the wider city unless there was a trial to be held or a formal decision to be made. They chose their new members in secret, and even their servants were sworn to secrecy. Of course, it helped that the servants of the Ilaria were all mechanical automatons—much like Pandaros—designed to keep the secrets of their masters.

Phoedius felt the cold weight of the Twelve's

disapproving eyes bear down on him, despite the fact that their eyes were buried behind silver hoods. But Phoedius knew they must be scowling beneath their cloaks.

He stood alone in the center of the courtroom. A ring of blood-red water separated him from the rest of the assembly —the trench made a perfect circle, turning the floor where Phoedius stood into a kind of island. Phoedius knew why the water was red: it was stained the color of blood to remind the accused that his life or death hanged in the balance. The guilty acolyte needed no reminding.

"Phoedius, child of Zeph and Xarien, you stand accused of crimes against the Physikos. How do you plead?" The booming voices of the Twelve rang out in unison. They sounded not like individual men and women but like a great voice of thunder, deep and heavy, filled with the sound of an oncoming storm.

Phoedius knew that no explanation, no excuse would save him from this judgment. After all, who would believe him? Who would believe that Merlin had the power to change his face, to be someone he was not? Merlin was surely gone anyway. Somehow Phoedius knew there would be no trace of him in the city.

Besides, Phoedius was guilty. He had betrayed his order, his empire, his own conscience. He had allowed the stranger Merlin into the very heart of the Physikos. What mercy could he possible plead? He did not mention the name of Merlin. He swallowed the name and let it rot in his stomach.

"Guilty." The word echoed out to the very walls of the chamber.

"Exile." The red waters rippled as if the earth was shaking.

"Send him to the outer reaches of the darkness."

"Alone."

"He shall keep watch and ponder his betrayal of the empire."

"He shall guard the ice planet and send back dispatches."

"He shall never return."

"He shall live out his days forever separated from the rest of the living."

"He shall be a stranger to us."

A stranger. Like the man who had come from the unnamed forests of the north and wielded the magic of the Old Realm. A stranger. Like the curly-haired youth with whom he had shared the depths of the ocean and the heights of the imperial city. A stranger.

That is what he had become. He would never rise to the rank of master now. He would never be one of the learned and powerful of the Physikos. The thought of it stung Phoedius's heart.

I am more ambitious than I realized, he mused as the guards took him away to the ship that would transport him to the ice planet. *And I was right about Merlin.* Phoedius couldn't help but find some self-satisfaction in remembering his initial suspicions of the mage. But those suspicions had all been for naught. Phoedius had succumbed and now he would pay the price.

Phoedius smiled to himself. How foolish the Council of Twelve had been. They should have sentenced him to death or to an eternity in the dungeons of the city. Instead, they had given him an unlikely gift. He almost laughed when he thought of what Merlin would say.

The ice planet. The farthest reaches of the known darkness. A world that had only been explored and studied by a few. It was uncharted. A world unknown.

And Phoedius would have a lifetime to discover it.

ALSO BY JENNIFER M. BALDWIN

The Thirteen Treasures of Britain (*Merlin's Last Magic Book 1*)

Ysbaddaden and the Game of Chess (*Merlin's Last Magic Book 2*)

Albion Reborn (*Merlin's Last Magic Book 3*)

Avalon Summer

Gates to Illvelion (*as A.R. Rathmann*)

Norse City Limits

ABOUT THE AUTHOR

Jennifer M. Baldwin lives with her husband and children in Michigan. She spends most of her days reading dusty old paperbacks, rolling 3d6 down the line, and wishing unicorns were real.

Visit her website: jmbaldwinwriter.com